Convincing Cole

Shore Thing Series

jaclynquinnbooks.com

Cover design by Designs by Morningstar Covers

Editing done by Anita Ford

Proofreading provided by Allison Holzapfel

Interior Design and Formatting provided by Flawless Touch Formatting

TRADEMARKS

DEDICATION

This is to all the readers who took a chance on me. You've helped make my dreams become a reality! Words can't express how much that means to me.

CHAPTER 1

COLE

"Cole, can you come to the front desk? We've got some *lovely* guests here who would like to speak to a manager," Miss Margie practically purred in her sweet-as-pie voice—the one she reserved for *lovely* guests—and abruptly hung up the phone. I sat there looking at the receiver in my hand and cursing under my breath. "Shit." What the hell happened now?

"You know better than to say you're leaving out loud. That's when the shit hits the fan." Levi tossed his pen on his desk, which faced mine in the small office we shared, and sat back in his chair. Selfishly, we'd made sure our office had an ocean view. One of the perks of living and working in paradise. "Did she say lovely?"

"Sure did. How'd I end up as Hotel Manager for the Coral Pointe Inn again? It's all a blur. Was I drinking? Can I take it back? I want a refund on my poor decisions." I slumped down in my chair and looked at the ceiling, shaking my fists above my head. "*Whyyyy?*"

Levi's shoulders shook, a rumble of a laugh rolling out of my so-called friend. "I'm pretty sure it's your sunny disposition. Or maybe it's your ability to spin shit into gold. Or because you're just so darn cute." He leaned forward, clasping his hands on the desk and quirked an eyebrow. "Or maybe…just maybe…it's because you take people's shit with a smile." Levi huffed. "We just came full-circle, didn't we? Poor decisions."

"I do not take people's shit." Except I did. I totally did. One person's in particular.

"Making sweet Miss Margie wait too long is a *really* bad decision. Almost as bad as the excuse you made up about what you're doing tonight. You know she can usually handle things on her own, so if she's calling you about *lovely* guests…" By *lovely*, of course she meant batshit crazy, pompous, impossible-to-please guests. Unfortunately, it wasn't good for business to call them all that to their faces. Shame.

I jumped up out of my chair, knowing all too well the truth in Levi's words—at least about making Miss Margie wait—slamming my knee into the desk in the process. "Sons a bitches!" Levi lamely offered to take care of it so I could leave, but I shot him the finger as I hobbled out of the office, hearing the jackass bark out a laugh behind me.

It had been a year since my best friends and I had the brilliant idea to open a hotel in Coral Pointe Inlet. A year since Levi found the listing in my childhood hometown for the inn foreclosure when he'd been working in commercial real estate. A year since we'd quit our respective jobs, pooled our savings to start Shore Thing Management, and moved to Coral Pointe in the hopes of 'living the dream.'

Don't get me wrong…we'd worked our asses off to get Coral Pointe Inn up and running over the last six months—still were—and there was no one I trusted more to do this with than my four best friends. But, for the love of Chris Hemsworth, if one more thing went wrong, I wouldn't be responsible for my actions. Because, surely, the crazy shit we dealt with—like calling animal control for a baby alligator a genius guest put in a bathtub or the cleaning crew opening the dresser drawers to find them full of oranges—didn't fall under the definition of *living the dream.*

Still, pride filled my chest as I walked down the hall to the ocean-breeze-filled lobby. Antique pine flooring stretched from the French entry doors to the reservation desk and down each modest wing of the twenty-nine room—because no way were we messing around with a room number thirteen—hotel. A cross-breeze from the front entrance to the beach and pool access exit cooled the lobby considerably in the Florida heat. Bamboo furnishings and comfy lounge-style seating in shades of coral, teal, and beige gave the space the laidback, Caribbean feel we were going for. Potted palms and tropical plants brought the calming outdoors in, blending the wraparound porch and the lobby into one cohesive design. It was our pride and joy. I kept telling myself that as I geared up for whatever the hell awaited me at the front desk.

"Sir, if you'll just wait a few more minutes, I'm sure he'll be—"

"Right here," I interjected, reaching my hand across the reservation desk in greeting. When it remained there, awkwardly hanging in the air without reception, I plastered a smile on my face and dropped my hand to the desk. *So, you're one of* those *guests, hmm?* "What can I do for you, Mr…?"

"Stafford. Mr. and Mrs. Stafford." Miss Margie wrung her hands together, worry creasing the dark skin around her eyes… and that just wouldn't do.

The disgruntled older man twisted his face into a scowl, his nervous wife standing at his side. "I was just telling your desk person—"

"Hospitality Clerk," I corrected, keeping that shit-eating grin on my face so as not to deck the condescending man.

"I beg your pardon?"

"Miss Margie is our Hospitality Clerk. We'd be lost without her." I could hear Miss Margie let out a breath beside me, her posture easing.

The man waved his hand in the air. "Whatever. I was telling her we were highly disappointed in our dinner last night. The shrimp was bland and the bread was like biting into Styrofoam."

Burke's gonna blow a gasket when he hears someone shit on his cooking. Can't. Fucking. Wait.

"I apologize that you had such a poor experience in our restaurant. I assure you, Oceanside Bar and Grill strives to serve our guests the finest cuisine on the Florida coast."

"Not *here*. My wife and I didn't travel all this way to eat subpar food in the hotel restaurant." *Oh no he didn't...* "She"—he rudely pointed at Miss Margie—"gave us a list of restaurants in the area, and I'm telling you the food at Bluefin was horrible."

Breathe, Cole. Breathe. "So, let me see if I'm understanding you. My Hospitality Clerk gave you a list of local restaurants, as she does as a courtesy for every guest who checks in, you chose a place from that list, and were unhappy with their food?"

The man gave a curt nod. "I'd like to know how we're going to be compensated for our troubles."

"Well, sir, if you'd like, I can contact the owner of Bluefin and make them aware of—" *What a supreme asshole you are.*

Mr. Stafford's gnarly pointer finger punctuated every other word on the desk as he made his disgust known. "I would like to know how *you* are going to reimburse me for *her* error!"

Now, listen, I'd always been a sensible guy, at least where business was concerned. There *was* a reason that, out of the five of us, I took on the task of Hotel Manager. By now, Burke would've shown this guy to his car by way of the front window, Levi would've yawned, completely unimpressed with the guy's tantrum, Ford would've nervously joked the whole thing off, and Noah would've escaped the situation altogether. I was the one least likely to lose my cool, even if I had the urge to grab the asshat by the collar of his Ralph Lauren polo and drag him out of the Coral Pointe for upsetting Miss Margie. No one—I repeat *no one*—was allowed to speak about sweet Miss Margie the way this jerk was.

"Mr. Stafford, I'm going to have to ask you to lower your voice so as not to disturb our other guests." I gave a polite nod and a gleaming smile to a couple leaving the hotel, whose curious looks said they'd heard at least part of this guy's rant. The disgruntled man scoffed, most likely about to spout off more insults, but I raised my voice. "Now, I'm sorry your dinner at Bluefin wasn't to your liking"—*Maybe the entitlement reeking from your pores fucked up your senses?*—"however, they are not affiliated with this inn directly. As a convenience, the town of Coral Pointe got together and made up a brochure for tourists, highlighting activities and local fare. Aside from our own inn, restaurant, and Shore Thing Tours, I'm afraid I have no control over your experience"—*or your pretentious, I-want-it-now tantrums*—"at another establishment. If you'd like, I can offer you a complimentary lunch in our—"

Veins bulging out of Mr. Stafford's neck, he slapped his hand down on the desk and spat, "This is outrageous! I demand to speak to a manager!"

Breathe in through the nose and out through the nose. "I *am* the manager, sir." Patience? Yeah, that left the chat five minutes ago.

"Then I want to speak to the owner." Beside the man, his wife shifted uncomfortably, looking back over her shoulder at the front doors as if planning her escape from her husband's embarrassing outburst.

I channeled my inner Kardashian and forced my biggest smile, reaching a hand out over the reservation desk. "Cole Sullivan, co-owner of the Coral Pointe Inn and Shore Thing Tours."

Oh, the look… You know the one—eyes bulging, mouth gaping like a guppy seeking air, floundering for a snarky comeback but failing miserably. Finally, he grumbled, "Well, as the *owner*, the least you can do is refund us for last night."

I'd officially had enough. "I'm afraid I can't do that, sir. Like I said, we'd be happy to give you both a complimentary lunch in our—"

Nostrils flaring, Mr. Stafford slammed his fist down hard on the counter this time, making both me and Miss Margie flinch. "Listen, you little—"

"Is there a problem here?" Not gonna lie, the deep timbre of Burke's voice to my left released tension in my shoulders I hadn't even been aware of. Yeah, I had a level head, but I also avoided physical confrontation like Superman avoided kryptonite.

Burke, however…

He crossed his arms over the wide expanse of his chest, his dark eyes narrowed beneath an equally dark furrowed brow, and his ever-present five o'clock shadow gave off that menacing look he'd been perfecting since college. "Seems to me we've offered more patience than you deserve, given how you just Hulk-smashed the counter I meticulously stained with my own two hands." Burke looked down, flexing those massive hands out in front of him before lifting hard eyes to Mr. Stafford. Thankfully, Burke was smart enough to move those hands to his hips because, let's face it…his glare was enough to make grown men whimper—and not in the way he got off on.

"You'll be hearing from my lawyer!" Mr. Stafford shouted, yanking his poor wife toward the front doors.

"Looking forward to it!" Burke retorted, getting another dirty look from Mr. Stafford. "We spent a pretty penny on our lobby cameras…complete with sound. I'd love to show them off."

"Let's go, Becky." Mr. Stafford pulled his wife along, mumbling curses along the way.

"Good riddance," Miss Margie breathed out. "Thank you, boys. You know I can hold my own, but I know when to throw in the towel and call in the big guns."

"Aw, then why'd you call Cole, Miss Margie?" Burke asked, kissing her on the cheek and making her laugh. She'd been my sixth grade teacher and had lived in Coral Pointe all her life, only a block from the inn. It just so happened she was looking for something to do because retirement was, as she said, *more boring than watching grass grow.* It had been a no-brainer hiring her with her sweet, welcoming smile.

"Hey." I shoved Burke aside, then flexed my biceps. "I've got big guns." Okay, so Burke's biceps looked like they ate mine for breakfast, but my lean muscle was hard earned, dammit.

Burke patted my cheek, his bottom lip pushed out into a pout. "Don't feel bad, Cole. Weapon dysfunction happens to the best of us. I mean, *I've* never experienced it, but I hear it's a thing."

I narrowed my eyes at another one of my so-called friends. Between him and Levi giving me shit today, I had two openings in the best friend category. Ford and Noah were already skating on thin ice and they didn't even know it yet. "You know, you and Levi can go jump—"

"Now, now, boys. I didn't ask you to calm one storm just so you could rile up another. Back to work." Miss Margie clapped her hands together twice, using that don't-even-think-of-disobeying-me voice she'd perfected over the years teaching smart-ass kids.

We were no fools. Burke and I both hung our heads and said, "Yes, ma'am."

Burke rubbed the top of his buzz-cut hair and sighed, lumbering off toward the kitchen. "I have soufflés to prepare." Only Burke could threaten a man with just a look and then go and bake something as delicate as a soufflé.

"Miss Margie, I'm done for the day. Levi's in the office if you need anything."

"Sure, honey. Everything's under control now." She gave me a soft smile then went about tidying the already-organized reservation desk.

Instead of leaving through the front doors, which led to the porte-cochère and valet, I meandered down the same hallway I had come from and out the back French doors onto the wraparound porch. The second my skin hit the warm, Florida air, I took in a deep, cleansing breath. I kicked my loafers off at the bottom of the wooden stairs and picked them up, following the path that ran alongside the pool and to the white sands of the beach that had always been home.

The decision to pack up and move back to Coral Pointe Inlet hadn't been a hard one. All I'd wanted after I graduated high school was to be out from under my mom's overprotective worrying. Paying off a student loan on the east coast had been cheaper than moving across the country to go to a school in California. Georgia had seemed like the best of both worlds—far enough away from my parents to live a little, but close enough to go home for holidays.

Ford and I met when we'd moved into the same dorm room freshman year. Burke and Levi had been next door, and Noah across the hall. After wrestling with and figuring out that we all waved the rainbow flag in one respect or another, our friendship solidified. For the next four years we'd been inseparable, even renting our own off-campus house together.

After living in Georgia for thirteen years, a stone's throw away from each other, the dream to open our own place on the beach started swirling around our brains. The guys had already been to my beachy hometown a few times, and we'd unanimously decided to set up shop there—which had pleased my mother to no end. It had taken a year to find the perfect place and another year to make it a reality. That perfect place happened to be on one end of the horseshoe that made up Coral Pointe, where the inlet met the ocean. But, as I gazed out at the blue water—heard the persistent call of the laughing gulls, breathed in the briny smell of the ocean, and felt the grainy sand between my toes and the gentle touch of the water as it glided over my feet before retreating—I knew I'd made the right decision to come home. *See, I can make good decisions, dammit.* Question was…who was I trying to convince?

My phone vibrated in my pocket, and I reached for it, pushing away the pang of disappointment as I looked at the screen and answered. "Why, hello there, Sage. What can I do for you on this beautiful day?"

"Don't you, 'hello there, Sage' me. What the hell is wrong with my bread?" Sage Rafferty demanded, his high-pitched tone piercing into the calm I'd built around myself. And, just like that, my mood lifted again.

"Apparently, it tastes like Styrofoam. You should really look into that. And, just a heads up, I know they're called packing peanuts, but I don't advise you use those in your peanut butter pie, either. You're welcome." I rolled my lips in, pressing my fist against my mouth.

"Are you fucking kidding me? Where is that asshole? I'll tell him where he can shove his sanctimonious sentiments about my—"

"Styrofoam?"

"Yes. NO!" Sage's anger slipped as he chuckled into the phone. "Jackass." His feisty mood seemed to deflate as he exhaled. "I make delicious shrimp, too, dammit."

"You make amazing shrimp. You know it, I know it, the whole town knows it. That guy wanted a comped room, end of story." It wasn't the first time and it wouldn't be the last, either.

"Yeah, well…sorry you had to deal with that. I don't know

who it was, but we didn't get a single complaint about a meal last night. To compensate you for getting your ass chewed out, you should send Levi over, and I'll make him the best shrimp he's ever had in his life."

"Wait…you're going to compensate *me* getting yelled at by feeding Levi a delicious dinner?" Leave it up to Sage to somehow turn this convo into a way to hit on Levi. Sage had all but camped out on Levi's front yard, naked, with a sign that read, *Fucking take me already*! The only one who seemed oblivious was my dear, sweet, clueless best friend.

But, let's face it, Levi could do worse than Sage. A hell of a lot worse. My habit of getting caught up in the web of the absolute wrong guy was something I was trying desperately to break. Did you ever read that quote by Warren Buffett? *Chains of habit are too light to be felt until they are too heavy to be broken.* When I'd read that a few weeks ago on some random social media post, I felt it in my soul. Nothing was heavier than the weight of a bad habit. Remember when I said I was level-headed? Yeah, well no one was perfect. I may have been smart enough to avoid physical confrontation, but Drake was a kryptonite I couldn't stay away from. Instead, I sought it out—him out—knowing what the ultimate outcome would be.

"Listen, sweets, I love you and all, but it's never gonna happen between us. There's too much cheer in your beer. I need a broody, dark stout. I need layers of creamy, rich flavor. I need—"

"Are we still talking about Levi? Because it sounds to me like you're trying to take a LandShark and disguise it as a Guinness." I pulled my feet out of the sand they had sunken into, leaving wells in their place that immediately filled with salt water.

"You laugh, but I know there's something brewing in that man. Lucky for him, I'm patient enough to wait for those flavors to meld together."

"Thanks, Sage. Now my pride is wounded and I'm thirsty." I

turned and headed south down the beach toward my place, leaving the tension from the earlier confrontation to blow away in the breeze.

Sage laughed into the phone. "No, seriously, I'm sorry you guys had to take the brunt of that. Come on by Bluefin tonight. There will be a decadent chocolate cake with your names on it. Hell, I'll even cut you the same size piece I give Levi."

"You're a giver, Sage."

"I know. It's a weakness."

"I've got plans tonight, though. Raincheck?"

It was never a good sign when Sage was silent. "Plans, huh?" When I responded with a sigh into the phone, he asked, "Where are you meeting him?"

I snorted. "What makes you think I'd tell you that?"

"It's a small town, Cole. I'll find out anyway."

I absolutely hated that he was right. We'd all exchanged privacy for paradise when we moved to Coral Pointe. "SandBar." I glanced across the inlet to the opposite end of the Coral Pointe horseshoe, hearing the faint music dance across the air from SandBar Brewing Co.

"Why do you do this to yourself?" Sage's voice softened, a tell that his concern was sincere.

"I'm not doing anything to myself, Sage. Drake and I have history"—*fuck that damn line about history repeating itself*—"but we're not exclusive." We weren't. He'd made me no promises. I could walk away anytime I wanted to. *Jesus, you make him sound like a drug.*

"But you would be in a heartbeat if he stopped dicking you around. I know you have history, but after the shit he pulled in college, and continues to pull, why do you let him treat you that way?"

The truth stung like a bitch, but I was in too deep now. Just like I had been back in high school. My parents weren't the only people I'd needed a break from when I'd graduated. Drake had graduated a year before me, and about six months into his freshman year, he'd dumped me to *expand his sexual horizons*. Seriously, who said shit like that? Neither one of us had been out back then, but I'd thought what we'd had was real.

I was stronger now, though.

I was.

Really.

"I gotta go, Sage." Because denial was easier than admitting I was getting in too deep—again. Reluctantly, Sage said goodbye. Of course, there was no *Have a good night* tacked on to that. Whatever. I didn't need anyone's blessing or permission, and I sure as hell didn't want anyone's unasked for advice or guilt.

I knew all too well about weaknesses. Except, instead of mine being a personality trait like Sage, it was a tall blond with commitment issues.

CHAPTER 2

AIDEN

"Hey, Aiden! Send another pitcher over, wouldya?" Marty, Coral Pointe's mail carrier and, as of an hour ago, the highest bowler on the Pointe Pin Heads bowling team, yelled over.

I laughed, watching the three men on the team—Carson from Wallace Auto Repair, Ziggy, the town's best electrician, and Marty—replay their games from today like they'd just won the Super Bowl. "Sure thing." I moved around the circular bar in the center of the concrete space, pitcher of our most sought after Flip Flops and Hops lager in hand, and walked it over to Marty's table. Slapping the older man on the back, I set the pitcher down with a laugh, listening to their antics.

Bob Marley's "Three Little Birds" floated in the air from speakers hanging in each corner of SandBar Brewing Co's tropical-meets-industrial bar. I'd made sure to have a space wide open with an oceanfront view so the salty air would recharge me on the daily. To my astonishment, a warehouse had opened up in the perfect spot where the inlet met the ocean. I had the best of both worlds: the quiet of the inlet to the right, and the breathtaking expanse of the Atlantic Ocean front and center. Picnic tables and standing bars with thatched roofs or teal umbrellas were scattered on the outside patio. Inside the warehouse-turned-bar, surfboards decorated the walls in an array of colors, TVs hung in strategic places, and thick, nylon boating rope wrapped around steel tables, stools, and the bar.

Cliché? Some would say so—namely *one*—but I didn't fucking care. This was my baby. SandBar Brewing Co had become a local and tourist hotspot in the three years since I'd opened. I'd already had the know-how to run a business after working at several bars in New York City and Rafferty's when I was younger, so I'd saved for years to make it happen. Now all I had to do was get old man Rafferty—otherwise known as Jim Rafferty, my pig-headed pop—to admit this place had turned into something great. Something we both could be proud of, if he'd just give it a chance. A place where Rafferty's and SandBar could be extensions of each other, not competitors. That had been my intention when I'd decided to move back to Coral Pointe: to showcase, not only the bolder brews I made now, but to proudly display Rafferty's tried and true favorites.

I was still waiting for that chance.

It had taken me a while to get my head out of my ass, to figure out that what was missing in my life was *home*—Coral Pointe, my family, my friends. When I'd moved back three years ago, Coral Pointe no longer felt like I was in a glass box without oxygen, like it had when I'd left eight years earlier. My old man hadn't been as outspoken as he'd once been, either, but that didn't mean he wasn't still stubborn as hell. Now he just used frowns instead of words. It took me a few weeks—longer than it should have—to realize the reason for his change was staring me right in the face.

He was bone-deep tired.

Deep down, I knew he didn't want to run the family business

on his own anymore. He cursed up a storm every time his once-agile body ached and fought against the things he'd done so easily when he was younger. Didn't change the fact that he was still a stubborn fool—hence the reason I'd left in the first place. I wanted to bring Rafferty's into the twenty-first century, and Pop refused to let go of tradition. Two stubborn jackasses and one business caught in the middle. Why couldn't he see that we could have the best of both worlds?

SandBar Brewing had its own spot in the town brochure, advertising a tropical escape people worked their whole week toward. Even if my pop refused to be a part of it, Rafferty's traditional brews, like Jim's Way IPA, would always have a place on our menu. I just had to buy the supply, like everyone else…with no family discount…and pick it up because Rafferty's didn't deliver. Did I mention how stubborn the man was?

But, over those eight years I'd been gone, I'd missed him something fierce. It would never be the same without my mom, but I wasn't giving up hope we could mend fences somehow.

I inhaled deeply through my nose, closing my eyes for just a second, breathing in the familiar scents of Coral Pointe. The ocean breeze definitely ranked high on my list of things I'd missed. I'd never get enough of it.

"You fallin' asleep over there, Aiden?" Marty said, elbowing me with a chuckle.

"Nah. Just getting my daily dose of salt in the veins. Good for the soul."

Marty let out a boisterous laugh. "Look at that! Somethin' you and your pop have in common other than being stubborn!" I let the sting of the comment roll off my back. The people who knew me and my pop well in this town wanted nothing more than to see us working together. They meant well. Still… "Now, I know he felt betrayed when you came back and started your own brewery, but isn't it time to bury the hatchet?" *In my fucking back? Thanks, Marty.*

I scoffed because it sure as hell hadn't been for my lack of trying. "Tell that to him, wouldya?"

I patted him on the shoulder and headed back inside behind the bar. Taking note of the crowd to make sure everything was covered, my eyes slid over to Cole for the tenth time that night. He'd been sitting there alone for an hour. It didn't take a genius to know who he was waiting for. Okay, so my cousin Sage had given me the heads-up, but when you owned a bar, you noticed patterns. Like, Rachel, a single mom, only came in on Thursday nights with her friends because that's when she could get a sitter; or my friend Jared, who owned and operated Bait and Switch, only ordered one beer on a Friday night because he opened his bait and tackle shop at the ass crack of dawn on Saturday mornings for all those eager fisherman.

Then there was Cole Sullivan. On the nights he came in alone and sat down at the bar inside, it only meant one thing: He was waiting for that asshole, Drake, to show up. And, if after twenty-minutes of him watching the entrance, the asshole didn't show up, I already knew Cole would be sitting there for another half hour to forty minutes by himself.

That's where owning a bar was hard as fuck. I saw and heard things all the damn time. Things that would make the town gossips jump for joy and skip down main street with megaphones. Luckily for half the people in this town, gossiping wasn't my thing.

It also meant I'd seen Drake the night before—and he sure as hell wasn't with the chestnut-haired, gloomy-eyed co-owner of the inn. No, he apparently didn't have a problem showing up for the barely legal, way-too-enthusiastic boy toy who'd made it clear within the first few minutes—with a shy pout that was fake as hell—that he *needed a fuck so bad, Drakey.*

I flexed my fingers, watching Cole stare into his beer, which had to be piss warm by now. Dicks like Drake Myers didn't deserve to have nice things. And, honestly, guys didn't come nicer than Cole Sullivan.

Hell, if I were gay, I'd go for a guy...like...Cole—where the hell did that come from? Was there such a thing as too much ocean air to the brain? Brain breeze?

I turned around and grabbed a new glass, pulling the tap for our Home of the Wave lager, and filled it to an inch from the rim. "Gimme that," I said, taking away the glass Cole had between both hands on the bar and sliding the fresh, cold beer in front of him.

Cole shook his head and pushed up from his stool. "No, it's cool. I should really get—"

I leaned my forearms on the reclaimed oak bar top. "Sit your ass down. It's on the house." When I was met with weary, blue eyes, I added, "Seriously, Cole. You wanna end this night on a crappy note or a *hoppy* one?" I wiggled my eyebrows. "See what I did there?"

Finally, for the first time since he'd come in, a smile curved his mouth. It didn't really reach his eyes, but...progress. "Shouldn't a bartender have better jokes than that?" he said, sliding back onto the stool.

I looked down at my watch. "Two hours ago I was on fire, but after being here for eight hours, all you get are the fading embers of my comedic brilliance."

Cole truly laughed that time, and man, the sound of it did funny things to me. I loved my job, loved talking with people, maybe making their day a little better. Knowing that he'd—*they'd...customers in general...of course*—laughed because of something I said was a fucking high like no other.

Cole and I hadn't really known each other before I'd left for college. When I'd graduated high school, he'd been thirteen and still in Coral Pointe K-8 with my cousin Sage. He'd only been back a year, but I'd gotten to know him and the guys through both Sage and working at the bar. Funny how five years didn't feel like such a difference in age as it had in our teens. Plus, as local business owners, we supported each other any way we could.

Realizing that Cole had a thing for Drake Myers became clear pretty quickly as I'd gotten to know him. Noticing that Drake Myers was a slimy, manipulative player had become crystal clear the second I had moved back to Coral Pointe.

"Wanna talk about it?" I asked, locking eyes with Cole to make it clear I'd listen.

Cole huffed. "Nope. Besides, I'm sure your cousin already called to warn you I'd be pathetically sitting at your bar *alone* tonight." He raised his beer. "To losers and lager." Then he took a huge gulp, wiping his mouth with the back of his hand. "Know how to break through tunnel vision? Cure acute stupidity?"

I straightened and grabbed an empty from the spot next to him, putting it in the bin to wash later. "You know why the phrase tunnel vision is even used? Because it's common. Because everyone has it at one point or another. You're not stupid, Cole. You're just…putting your energy into the wrong damn guy." He flinched, but it needed to be said, for fuck's sake. I knew the guys, his four best friends, had told him before. Even Sage had given his opinion. Hell, it was impossible for Sage *not* to give his opinion. But, maybe Cole needed to hear it from someone else. Someone who had his eyes and ears on half the town on a daily basis.

Me.

He needed to hear it from *me*, dammit, because my desire to punch the arrogant bastard—who'd stood him up again—in the face was growing like a living, breathing thing inside me every time Cole put himself down.

"What is it about him?" The question surprised even me, but

once the words left my mouth, I realized I really wanted to fucking know. What was so damn special about Drake that made a nice, successful, and…all right, I could admit it…good-looking guy go through all this shit time after time?

He laughed, a bitter huff lacking any humor. "I'm not even sure I know anymore." He took another drink and shrugged. "I guess part of it is history. He was my first everything, ya know? We'd only been out to each other at that point, confided our biggest secrets." He exhaled, resting his right elbow on the bar with his head cradled in his hand. "Maybe a small part is about trying to fix what I did wrong."

"What *you* did wrong?" Was he kidding?

"Well, he broke up with me for a reason, right? Things weren't bad between us until he went to college. Probably because I had no clue what I was doing when it came to sss…" He widened his eyes and sat up straight. "Jesus Christ, why am I telling you all this shit? As if I don't look pathetic enough." He blew out a breath, pointing a finger at me. "Just to make it clear, I know what the hell I'm doing now."

I barked out a laugh, watching his face flush again. "Good thing."

"No issues with…*you know*."

"Got it. *You know* is in working order." I gave him a wink and the universal sign for okay.

He slumped and shook his head. "I'm just gonna shut up now."

I leaned on the bar again in front of him. "Listen, I'm gonna tell you what I learned when I got divorced." Which had been hell, at first, until Sasha and I woke the fuck up and admitted it was definitely for the best. "You can't change someone to fit your expectations."

"So, what you're saying is, I'll never meet his expectations? Good to know."

I grabbed his hand, the feel of it in mine surprising me. When we simultaneously looked down at our joined hands, I immediately let go, dropping mine to my side, flexing my tingling fingers. "That's not what I meant. You can't change Drake into someone who suddenly doesn't treat you like shit. He's the one not meeting your expectations, Cole. Not the other way around."

Cole sucked in a breath, pulling at the collar of his short-sleeve, light blue button down and glanced around, and it hit me that I'd said Drake's name a little too loudly. It wasn't like people in the town didn't know or anything, but still, I was never one to call out someone's shit in the middle of the bar. Luckily, the bar was winding down, and most patrons were outside now. His blue eyes flicked back to me, the tanned skin of his cheeks flushing pink, and I cleared my throat and added, "Sorry. It's just…I don't get it. All you've done tonight is blame yourself and put yourself down. You're better than that, man. It pisses me off that you can't see he's the dumbass here, not *you*."

He took another slow sip of his beer, but I saw the smallest smile on his lips as they touched the rim of the glass. *I'm noticing the strangest shit tonight.*

Cole's eyes dropped, focusing on the bar. "You sound like the guys," he finally said, lifting those eyes to look back at me and giving me a half smile.

"Shouldn't that tell you something?"

He stared at me for a couple of seconds and, to be honest, I just froze. Maybe I'd gone too far? Hell, I wasn't one of his closest friends. I was the *cousin* of a friend. The guy who was five years older and straight to boot. What the hell did I know about—

"Thanks. I think I needed to hear it again." He rubbed his hands on his thighs, glancing around. "You need any help cleaning up?" When I opened my mouth to say no thanks, he tacked on, "I could really use the distraction, and…I don't really feel like going home right now." There was something in the way he said it that made me think there was another reason he didn't want to go home, but I let it drop.

I gave a short nod, finding it hard to say no to Cole with that damn sad look he was giving me. "Wanna grab the empties from the tables outside?" Something like relief transformed his pained expression as he pushed up from the stool.

We worked in silence for another hour, and I just let him do his thing. I understood all too well how hard it was to admit to yourself that what you were desperately trying to hold on to wasn't worth it. Sasha and I had tried for a couple of years to make our marriage work. Counseling, planning date nights—hell, we even started to schedule *sex*. We were a fucking mess. The hardest part, though, at least for me, was feeling like I'd failed. I'd walked away from the family business, moved to New York, married a girl my family had never met and I had next to nothing in common with—except the sex. The sex was off the fucking charts when we'd first met—until we'd tried to turn that into something more. Bad idea.

After an expensive divorce and a move back home? Yeah, lesson fucking learned.

But, as I looked around this place that I'd poured my heart and soul into—covered in blood, sweat, and tears—I knew I'd made the right decision three years ago.

"Hey…so I think you're pretty good out there now." Cole shoved his hands in the pockets of his shorts. "I'm gonna head out."

I gave him a big grin and leaned back against the counter behind me. "Thanks. Saves me some time tonight. Netflix, here I come."

Cole let out a short laugh and turned away, only to stop a couple of steps later. He faced me again, biting his bottom lip, then said, "Thanks…for talking with me. It made things a little easier tonight." There was something vulnerable in those words, and that struck a chord with me so loud it rang in my ears.

I wanted to say I'd been there. That things would get better. But, let's face it…that never worked. He was the only one who could stop this shit from happening over and over again. So, what I ended up saying instead was, "Anytime, man."

It wasn't until I said the words out loud that I knew I truly meant it.

CHAPTER 3

COLE

Sunday nights weren't usually when other businesses held their meetings but for us, it was the only time we could. Ford and Noah finished early at Shore Thing Tours, and the inn was usually slow. Well, slower than the rest of the week. With the hire of a new part-timer at the front desk, we were able to hold the meetings at one of our places while one of us stayed on-call. The first rule we'd made when we started the business was never work too much that we lost our friendship because, bottom line, the bond the five of us had was too important.

Once we covered everything about the business, we just hung out. That was also a rule: Separate places. There was no way we could work with each other all day *and* live together. We were as close as brothers, but everything had its limits.

So, finding ourselves holding a meeting at SandBar was unusual. Fine, it was my idea, but only because, for the first time in a long time, SandBar didn't feel like it was tainted.

I'd been going stir-crazy at night by myself. My *poor decisions* tried to chatter me into some bad shit every time Drake texted me. His lame excuse for standing me up the other night had been that he'd had to work late.

Heard that one before.

It had been a few days since then, and honestly, I was fucking proud of myself for not caving. Bonus reason for being at Sand-Bar: I thought seeing Aiden again would help keep me on track, because even though I knew I was being used, my body didn't fucking care. It was my heart and mind that I had to deal with in the aftermath of the shitstorm that was Drake Myers. My friends had been lecturing me for several months to toss Drake aside, but there was something about Aiden's raw honesty that made me re-examine what the hell I was doing.

I glanced around the bar for the hundredth time, wondering why it mattered that Aiden wasn't working tonight.

"You get that shit on my shirt, I break your face." Burke glared pointedly at the offensive ketchup bottle making obscene noises as Ford tried to squeeze more out onto his burger.

To most people who saw Burke's size, that threat might have had them cowering in fear.

To us…?

"Uh oh. Burke's cranky. Quick, someone get him another beer." Ford snapped his fingers.

Noah threw his hand in the air. "Jesse, we need a Jim's, STAT!" He patted Burke on top of his shaved head, Jesse laughing and giving him a salute. Noah, just to piss Burke off even further, added with a sympathetic smile, "It's okay, little guy…she's getting your bottle ready." That simple smile turned into a shit-eating grin, the rest of us laughing around mouthfuls of food.

"Funny," Burke snapped, reaching for the bottle Jesse was handing to him, a smirk breaking through his façade. He looked up at Jesse and shook his head. "Don't encourage them."

The conversation turned back to work, but not in the business sense of the word. Sometimes, we just needed to vent about the crazy shit we had to deal with.

"Damn, I earned this burger today. Teaching someone who's terrified of water how to paddleboard? Not so fun. I spent most of the hour convincing her to release her death grip on the board and put it in the water. Then I had the kids' camp, and *then* some punk-ass teens who felt like they didn't need the surf lesson their mom signed them up for. Needless to say, they drank more water than they surfed." He let out a long exhale and shook his head.

"Did someone puke all over your favorite sneakers today? No? Then quit your whining. I can't even eat." Noah griped, staring down at the onion ring in his hand with a wrinkled nose, tossing it back down onto his plate. Mumbling under his breath, he added, "Who has a large chocolate milkshake right before they go on a boat? Ruined my red Sauconys."

"Not the red ones!" Burke threw a hand to his chest, eyes wide and mouth gaping.

Noah laughed, chucking an onion ring at Burke who skillfully looped it onto his finger in mid-air. "Shut up. Let's see you try to eat while thinking about chunks swimming in milkshake on your *shoes*."

"Dude, that was so fucking funny." Ford wiped tears from his eyes, his laughter dying down. "You're right. You win."

Levi sighed, clanking his fork down onto the plate next to his half-eaten baked potato. "Thanks for that."

"Doesn't bother me. I've been dreaming about this burger all day." Ford pressed his burger tightly between his fingers, maneuvering the greasy, fat sandwich to take an enormous bite. The guy ate like a fucking Hoover. He loved food almost as much as he loved sex—he wasn't picky about the variety of either.

Burke lifted a menacing eyebrow, eyes locked on Noah as he shoved the entire onion ring in his mouth.

My phone buzzed in my pocket and I pulled it out, Ford's

words getting fainter and my palms sweating as I read the text from Drake.

I can be at your place by nine.

Was he serious? And why the hell did my heartbeat immediately kick into overdrive the second I heard from him? I'd been so good. Days had passed and he acted as if I hadn't ignored all his texts. **I'm with the guys.**

Fine then. Nine-thirty.

I blew out a breath, feeling my resolve slipping away faster than a sloth down an oil-slicked hill, my hands shaking as I tried to think of something clever to type. He must have taken that silence as me ignoring him. Which was funny, since I'd never played hard to get in my whole damn life.

Come on. Don't be that way, babe.

Babe? He'd never called me that before. Heart-pounding hope flared in my chest from that one fucking endearment. There was no bright light at the end of the graffiti-ridden tunnel as it sprang up around me. Nope, just me and my withering willpower.

Fine. Just another fucking word, but it was heavy as I tried desperately to carry it. Shoving the phone back in my pocket, I felt my stomach plummet. Because instead of telling Drake I'd had enough…instead of telling him not to call me fucking *babe*, I chose to tell him *fine*. I'd given him the damn green light.

Silence fell over the table and I looked up, seeing all eyes on me. "I don't wanna talk about it," I sighed, before any of them could open their damn mouths.

"Yep. That about answers that question." Burke crumpled up his napkin and tossed it on the table next to his plate.

"What an asshole," Ford said, then took another huge bite of his condiment-smothered monstrosity.

"Him or me?" *Dammit.* My shoulders tensed as I looked away and, beyond my comprehension as to why, scanned the crowded bar and restaurant for raven hair and a teal SandBar polo. Something bounced off the side of my neck and landed on the table in front of me. "What the hell?" I glared at all four of them until Ford held up one figure as he swallowed the bite he'd taken.

"Sorry, I was aiming for your face." The smartass took a swig of beer, a smug brow lifted.

I huffed out a laugh. "You were a quarterback with that aim?"

Completely ignoring the dig, he replied, "You know, when Drakeula shows up at your door, he can't come in unless you invite him. It's Vampire 101."

"Yes. Thank you, Ford!" Levi smacked his hand down on the table with a loud thud, drawing gawking looks from the people around us at neighboring tables. He, out of all of us, was the most serious-minded. To some, he came off as a bit of an uptight asshole, but with us, he was the Levi people didn't get to meet. The guy needed to learn how to loosen up, and Coral Pointe was just the place to do that. Given half the chance, Sage would untie those knots in his shoulders and find more creative ways to use the rope. His words, not mine. But Levi was blind to what was going on right in front of him. *Pot meet kettle...*

"Alright, leave the guy alone." The deep baritone behind me caught me off guard, making me jump seconds before a big, warm hand landed on my shoulder. Mere minutes before, I'd been looking for him, and now I was embarrassed at the obligatory best-friend scolding I was stuck in the midst of—that he'd undoubtedly heard.

"Hey, Aiden," Noah said first followed by a string of hellos from everyone else. "Grab a chair and sit down. I'm guessing by your Pink Floyd T-shirt you're off tonight?"

Chair legs screeched on the cement floor, Aiden taking up space right beside me, radiating heat from his larger frame. My stomach coiled, the guilt of what I'd already agreed to tonight trying to eat its way out of my stomach like Ford just devoured that burger. Shit. I was fucking hopeless, and I knew it. I'd come here all proud of myself for ignoring a few measly texts, only to cave five minutes later.

Whatever.

I didn't owe anyone an explanation. *Except yourself, asshole.*

"Yeah. Just came in to do payroll." He reached over, stealing a fry off my plate and popping it into his mouth. My eyes followed the movement of his strong jaw followed by the bob of his Adam's apple, and I practically swallowed my tongue. He wasn't even my type—*because you prefer the fuck and run type?*—but I wasn't blind for fuck's sake. The man was hot as hell. Thick, coal-black hair cut short, peppered with a few strands of gray; green eyes that popped against his tan skin; a perfectly plump mouth in the center of dark, sexy stubble.

And straight.

Jesus Christ, what was I doing? I'd officially fallen into creepy territory, eyeing my straight friend like he was my next meal. Wasn't it bad enough I was addicted to an asshole? Did I really have to stoop even lower?

It hit me a second later that the mouth that had just devoured the fry was moving, Aiden's eyes on me.

"Huh?"

Those lips parted in a gleaming-white smile, his shoulder nudging mine. "I asked if you're okay."

"Oh, uh…yeah. Yeah, I'm good." My phone felt like it weighed fifty pounds in my pocket. "Just tired, I guess."

He eyed me for a second, his mouth opening then snapping shut again in what looked like hesitation. Aiden's eyes scanned the table, and I followed their route, seeing the other guys involved in some other conversation about who the hell knew what. When those green orbs landed back on me, I tensed up, not sure if it was scrutiny or intensity I saw in them. "What about the, uh…tunnel?"

Aiden flicked his gaze once more to the group, but they were too busy arguing over jellyfish and the effectiveness of pee stopping the sting…as one should at the dinner table…right after a discussion about vomit…in the middle of a crowded restaurant. That was what happened in a group made up of guys. At least, in our group it did.

I was pretty sure Edna Lawry at the next table over did *not* agree, judging by the cutting glare she was aiming our way with her laser-red eyes. Okay, they were brown, but man, I was pretty sure they were going to burn a hole right through the back of Ford's head any minute now. Of course, Edna's expression defaulted to glare as a general rule. I'd learned a long time ago, back when I was still living with my parents next door to Mrs. Lawry, that pretty much everything pissed her off—my soccer ball too close to her yard, my dad's orange tree grazing her fence, the TV on at night while the windows were open.

Edna Lawry was a *peach*.

A warm thigh pressed against mine under the table, the faint tickle of leg hair as it whispered against mine. Maybe my weakness toward Drake wasn't about him at all. Maybe I was just fucking horny. Why else was I suddenly finding it hard to breathe? Why the hell else was my cock swelling beneath my shorts. Reading the intensity in Aiden's eyes—or confusing the heat from his thigh still pressed against mine—as anything other than concern was almost as stupid as giving in to Drake time and time again.

"The *tunnel*?" he repeated, but I could tell by the faintest flash of pity in his eyes that he already knew the answer, so why not just tell him the damn truth?

"Still stuck in the middle waiting for that supposed light to spit my ass out the other side." I gave him a small smile and a shrug.

He returned the smile but didn't say anything else, an understanding flowing between us. I got enough shit from the guys. I knew I was fucked. He knew I was fucked. I didn't need the reminder.

"Cole, check's on you tonight." Levi handed me the bill and I took it, pulling my wallet out of my pocket.

"I'll take it over to Jesse," Aiden said, holding his hand out for my card. "Be right back." A minute later he came back with a copy to sign, then handed me my card with my copy of the receipt.

"Thanks." I stood up and shoved them both in my pocket.

The others, having said their goodbyes, were already to the door and deep in another debate.

I stared at Aiden for a second then said, "I'll see you later." I wasn't sure why I felt compelled to say it. Something inside me knew I needed to make a change. I needed to start giving a shit about things that mattered to me. Being a part of this community, my friends, my family…they all mattered to me, and I'd been half-assing it for a few months now.

Aiden gave a soft smile that absolutely did *not* make my belly flutter. "See ya."

As I walked toward the door, something compelled me to look back over my shoulder. Aiden still stood there, hands in the pockets of his shorts, impassive look on his face as he stared back at me. I swear I felt the prickle of his eyes on me all the way home.

An hour and a half later, my doorbell rang, and I exhaled long and slow before opening the door.

"Hey, babe." Drake swooped in, his arms going around my waist.

There was that word again. It had always meant something to me in other relationships…until now. Now it just felt out of place. *Because this isn't a relationship.* My stomach chose to ignore that little tidbit and flipped as I looked him over. He was wearing a tight, navy blue tee over lean, golden muscles and worn jeans that always hugged his ass just right. His blond hair was disheveled in that just-ran-my-hands-through-it style, even though I knew how long it actually took him to perfect it every day. His deep blue eyes—eyes that had left me breathless since high school—studied me as he waited for a proper greeting.

"Hey," was all I could muster in that moment. I already knew what his hands felt like on my body, his lips on mine, the way he could turn me inside out. But, did I know who he really fucking was? Nope. I got the Cliff's Notes version. The façade. *The player.* My stomach flipped again, except this time it left me feeling like I was going to lose my dinner.

"I knew you'd come around. We're so good together, Cole." His deep voice never failed to send a shiver down my spine.

Those words from him made my breath hitch. If we were so good together, why was it such a big deal to be exclusive? I opened my mouth, digging deep for the courage to just ask him.

Until he opened his mouth again.

"We always are." He thumbed my bottom lip, pulling it down. "No one has a mouth like you." *No one.* Meaning, none of the other guys he was fucking. Was that his version of a compliment? Drake smacked me on the ass then headed toward my bedroom, pulling his shirt over his head as he went. "I don't have long. Have to be up early tomorrow for a meeting." Which also meant he wasn't staying. He'd be out the door before the sweat chilled my skin.

I reached in my pockets, pulling my wallet out of my back pocket and the card and receipt from dinner from my front pocket. It wasn't until I separated the card from the receipt that I saw words written on the back. Flipping the thin slip of paper over, my fingers trembled as I read the scribbled print underneath a phone number.

. . .

If you ever need to talk
or a flashlight…
A

Aiden had given me his number. A freight train ran through that dark tunnel, knocking the breath right out of me. He'd known I was going to mess up tonight, and he was willing to lend an ear *again.*

"Babe, what are you doing?" Drake stood in my hallway, completely fucking naked, hands on his hips right over where they dipped into a V, a scowl on his gorgeous face, and his hard cock bobbing in front of him. I couldn't deny the way my body was reacting, how my cock lengthened or my mouth watered, seeing all that smooth skin on display. Skin I had tasted and touched.

But, even stronger was the queasy feeling that dropped like a bowling ball in my stomach again. This was all this was ever going to be. All I was to Drake was an eager mouth and a tight hole. Disgust raced down my spine, its harsh fingers aiming directly at all my weaknesses—my inability to have a fucking backbone.

I dropped my gaze to the small slip of paper in my trembling hand, tears clouding my vision as I read the words again. "You need to go," I whispered, still not meeting Drake's eyes.

"What?" Drake huffed out a laugh, stalking toward me, confidence in his swagger, and unabashed vanity in every naked step.

I backed up as he moved toward me, lifting my eyes to his even though embarrassment burned my face. My back hit the front door, my hand flying up between us, pressing on his hard chest so he couldn't come any closer. My skin knew the heat of his, but my heart shoved the unwelcome feeling away. I drew in a breath and straightened my spine. "You need to go." Somehow, the words had come out firmer, stronger, and the power in that was surprising.

"What the hell are you talking about?"

"I can't do this anymore, Drake." I sucked in a shaky breath. "I'm never going to be enough for you, am I?" My fist curled around the thin piece of paper in my hand, drawing strength from the scratch of blue ink on it.

Drake groaned in frustration, rolling his eyes. "Cole, do we have to go through this again? It's sex. It's not complicated. It's not life or death." His hand began a downward trajectory, and damned if my traitorous cock didn't respond, but thank fuck my hand was quicker. I grabbed his wrist and yanked it away.

"It's not complicated for you, because you don't give a shit who you hurt. Well, it's complicated for me." I shoved him hard enough for him to take a few wide-eyed steps back, his mouth gaping. It was enough time to take a deep breath and stomp around him.

I rushed down the hall, picking up the bastard's discarded clothes along the way, finding the last few pieces in my bedroom on the floor. With the pile in my hands, I rounded the door back into the hall, took several large steps to him, and shoved the ball of clothes against his chest. There was no surprise in his eyes this time. No, this time I could see the smoke coming out of his ears.

He dropped the clothes on the floor and picked up only his boxer briefs, slowly putting them on with a smug sneer. "You know, this is why it never worked out between us all those years ago. I needed more, and quite honestly, you're right—you weren't enough. You may have a fantastic mouth now, but"—his empty eyes raked down my body leaving a chill in their wake—"the rest leaves something to be desired." Next piece of clothing was his jeans. "I finally had to break up with you, because what else was I gonna say? *Can you fuck me like the guy who works in the campus bookstore does? Can you stop being such a prude and suck my damn cock like you mean it or fucking* swallow *for a change? Because the dude across the hall from me has no issues.*" He scoffed.

My blood ran cold. I'd always had a feeling he'd cheated on me, but that fucking stung worse than a slap to the face.

"At least you've perfected your cocksucking skills." He laughed bitterly, dragging his tee over his head. After pulling on his shoes, he opened the door, pausing in the doorway. "Sex is sex, Cole. It's not fairytales and hearts and happily-ever-afters. When you grow the hell up, give me a call. I don't have time for your ridiculous expectations, but I'll make time for that mouth."

I flinched as the door slammed behind him, reverberating off the walls like a shotgun blast. I stared at the door for what felt like hours after he'd left. What the hell had I just done? Was I making this a bigger deal than it needed to be? Obviously, there were plenty of guys out there ready and willing for a quick, no-strings-attached fuck.

My hands shook, my heart pounding with every step toward the couch. I dropped down on it, covering my eyes with my forearm to block out the harsh ceiling light.

I don't have time for your ridiculous expectations...

"Fuck!" Great, now that was going to play over and over again in my head. I felt the crinkle of the paper still crushed in my hand, and I rushed to open it, hoping I didn't smear the ink with my sweaty palm. My fingertips ran over the words, bringing to mind others that Aiden had said.

You can't change someone to meet your expectations...

He's the one not meeting your expectations, Cole. Not the other way around.

With a deep exhale, I pulled my phone out of my pocket and plugged in the number. Talking felt like too much too soon. Drake's words had shredded me raw, and I knew the evidence of it would be in my voice. So, instead, I texted… **Thanks for the flashlight.**

The reply was immediate. **Wasn't sure you'd see that.** There was a pause and then… **Anytime.**

I thought for a moment, laughing as I typed…**My vision's been compromised.**

His response of, **Welcome to life outside the tunnel**, made a knotted thread loosen in my chest, because he'd gotten my meaning.

I smiled at the screen, feeling lighter already. **Thanks again…** I stood up, heading down the hall to my room when my phone buzzed again.

Get some sleep. Gotta head off all those early bird, senior speed walkers in the morning.

I didn't think I would laugh tonight, but there it was. **Don't have to be there till ten.**

There was an even longer pause, those three little dots teasing at the bottom of the screen. I closed my eyes after seeing my bed unmade and grasping the reason why. *Gonna have to change my sheets, dammit.* I flinched when the phone vibrated in my hand.

I'll be at the marina at seven for a run. In case you need to blow off some steam.

My fingers hovered over the keyboard, a smartass remark about that being my only strong suit ready to fire off. Luckily, I had the common sense to remember this was not one of the guys, but Aiden, who definitely was *not* into guys sucking cock. **Pretty sure the Walkie Talkies will be more alert than me at that hour.**

You gonna let Irma show you up?

I snorted a laugh, picturing the eighty-five year old grandmother in her bright pink shorts and T-shirt, and an enormous visor that had been assaulted by way too many flowers on her head.

Yup, I typed, but I wasn't sure that was my final answer. The real decision maker would be if I was able to get any sleep.

LOL Night, Cole.

Night.

I wasn't positive—it wasn't like I had a mirror over my bed—but I was pretty sure, after all that had happened with Drake, I'd still fallen asleep with a smile on my face.

CHAPTER 4

AIDEN

The marina was quiet on Monday mornings, just the way I liked it. A light breeze off the Atlantic Ocean swept through my hair thanks to the mild spring temperatures. All too soon, humidity would inflate the air, making the summer months hot as hell. It had taken me a while to get acclimated again to the weather in sunny Florida after living in NYC, but I sure as hell didn't miss the snow or frigid temps of a Northeast winter.

My muscles were already warmed up from the walk over, making stretching each muscle a little easier. My agile mind wanted to deny what my thirty-eight-year-old body couldn't: If I didn't stretch out before a run, I'd be in bad shape later, which totally defeated the purpose of exercising to begin with. I pressed my fingers over my ribs as they mocked me, reminding me of the time I sneezed wrong and cracked one. I still had no idea how the hell I had managed that one.

"Those Walkie Talkies mean business. Irma almost took me down crossing Sea Turtle Drive."

I looked back over my shoulder, a huge smile breaking

through, surprised to see Cole had actually taken me up on my offer. "Why do you think I pick up the boardwalk from here? From seven to eight every morning, those gossiping grannies rule the streets."

Cole snorted, rubbing his hands on his track shorts. "You weren't kidding. I miss all the excitement running at night."

There was an awkward pause, both of us staring at each other. Up until last week, Cole and I hadn't hung out on our own. I couldn't for the life of me figure out why. Since moving back to Coral Pointe, I really only had two close friends, and one of those was my cousin Sage. Jared was the only other person I'd hung out with on the regular, and even then, it was mostly on nights when he came into the bar.

Cole looked around, an uneasy expression tightening his brow. "So, uh…I guess I'd better stretch out first unless I want to hobble around the inn during my shift."

"Yeah. Same." Holy hell, why was this so uncomfortable? It was just Cole for fuck's sake. We weren't close, but we sure as hell weren't strangers.

Cole bent at the waist, reaching down for a hamstring stretch, the muscles in his thighs and calves flexing with the movement. He was obviously accustomed to exercise and keeping his body strong and healthy. He switched to the other side, the material of his black shorts stretching across—

I cleared my throat, shifting my eyes and body away. *What the hell are you doing?* Shaking my limbs to loosen the tension, I lunged my left foot forward, bending at the knee, my left forearm braced on my thigh while my right hand stretched overhead. I'd been a runner all my life, learning how to stretch my body properly on the high school track team. I let my mind focus on my warm muscles, inhaling the salty air that, I swear, made up part of my DNA. It cleared my mind like nothing else could.

Muscles warmed up and ready, I turned around and found

myself watching Cole again. He reached back, his right leg bent back at the knee while he gripped his foot behind him, stretching out his hip flexor. The soft, black material of his shorts stretched against a different part of his anatomy this time. Blood pumped loud and fast through my ears, trying its best to reach other places. Quickly, I looked up at the blue sky and dragged in another deep breath, pushing away confusion trying to cloud my mind.

It didn't shock me that I was noticing these things about Cole. For the past few days, I'd been trying to figure out what the hell Cole saw in Drake, but it was obvious to me what Drake saw in Cole. Of course, that had led my mind in another direction, because if Drake kept coming back to Cole's bed time and time again, it was obviously for a reason. Which then led my imagination down roads it didn't belong because, let's face it, I didn't know the first thing about gay sex.

Well, that wasn't entirely true. I mean, anal sex was anal sex right? Sasha had been up for anything when we'd first met. So, being with Cole couldn't be that different from—*whoa. Whoa. Whoa. Whoa. Back it the hell up, Aiden.*

"You ready?" Cole's deep voice made me jump, and I had the ridiculous fear that he'd somehow read my mind. What would he say if he knew the thoughts that had just bounced through my head like an aggressive game of ping pong? "Aiden?"

"What? I mean, yeah. Let's do this."

After a few minutes, my body fell into that familiar rhythm, blood pulsing through my veins, breath releasing in steady exhales, muscles warm. This was my favorite time of day. The knowledge that there was someone next to me—sharing every breath I took, feeling the adrenaline coursing through their veins at the same time it coursed through mine, their body also sweating from the heat—was oddly exhilarating.

Only one other physical activity I could think of felt even better than this.

Focus, Aiden.

We ran in silence around the inlet, passing familiar sights and sounds of Coral Pointe in the morning. No doubt Noah and Ford were getting Shore Thing Tours open and ready for the day. A charter boat from Coastal Catch left wakes trailing behind as Rick brought out a handful of people on the morning fishing trip. He waved in our direction and we both waved back. It was one of the many reasons I loved Coral Pointe. The inn came into view, signaling the end of the boardwalk and our cue to turn around and head back toward the marina.

After the run ended, I had the common sense to look away from Cole as we stretched our pulsing muscles, but I was inept at examining the reason *why* I needed to focus on something else. Was I that starved for human contact? I hadn't been with anyone since…longer than I cared to figure out…and even those hookups were random one-offs.

"I should get going. I want to stop by the bakery and get some pastries for the breakroom." Cole linked his hands together and stretched them above his head, a sliver of golden skin peeking out between his gray tee and black shorts.

Again, I looked away, shifting my eyes to the sky. "Yeah, I gotta get over to my pop's and pick up my order."

"How's he doing?" Cole asked, but I understood the underlying question.

I dropped my gaze back down and shook my head with a snort. "He's as stubborn as usual. I don't think that's ever going to change."

"That can't be easy." Cole looked at me with concern.

My shoulders slumped, a long exhale leaving my lips. I could say what I said to everyone else—that I didn't care. I could shrug as if it wasn't a big deal and pretend it didn't get to me. As I looked at Cole, the words just came out. "All I can do is continue to support him while working my ass off to make SandBar a success. I keep hopin' one day he'll come around and realize I didn't do this to spite him. I did it because…" I blew out another breath and glanced around at the boats, searching for the right words.

"Because you needed to follow your dreams. If you didn't, you'd always have a what-if standing between you and your dad regardless. Look at what you've built. It's amazing, Aiden. You should be proud."

My head snapped Cole's direction, feeling seen for maybe the first time since moving back home. Sure the rest of the town was coming around, but even though SandBar was doing well, I wasn't naïve. I wasn't deaf to the whispering I knew was going on behind my back. A topic of conversation for the Walkie Talkies. Words like *disrespect* and *ashamed* and *poor Jim*… Those people had no clue what they were fucking talking about. They had no clue that I'd fought long and hard to be an equal part of the family business. They had no clue how many sleepless nights I'd had and was still having.

But Cole knew.

I swallowed the lump in my throat, the air humming between us. "Thanks, man."

Cole gave me a small, somewhat shy smile, his cheeks flushing. "Anytime," he said, repeating back to me what I'd said to him the other night.

It felt like a beginning. To what, I wasn't sure, but something was brewing. Maybe he could be the friend I'd been needing since moving back. Sage was a part of my family, and it wasn't fair to get him involved. Jared had his own family shit to deal with. He didn't need to try and wade through mine too. A small voice niggled in the back of my mind, telling me Cole already had his group…his ride-or-die friends. Still, there was something in his blue eyes that enticed me to see if he was someone I could confide in.

"I go in late again on Thursday. Same time, same place?" Cole ran a hand through his sweat-soaked, chestnut hair.

"I'll be here." I waved as Cole nodded once and turned to walk away.

Gripping my hips, I stared back out at the inlet, to the ocean beyond. An off-kilter feeling ate at me until I found myself outside Bait and Switch. Knowing what had brought me here and admitting it out loud were two completely different things. I wouldn't bother Jared with family shit, but this...*this* he could give me some insight on. This strange connection I was beginning to feel toward Cole. A fusion between reactions I normally only had with women and a building friendship with Cole. I couldn't make heads or tails of it. Hell, I couldn't even figure out if I was blowing it out of proportion.

"You gonna stand out there all day or ya comin' in?" Jared drawled, leaning his forearms on the counter as he stared out the tackle shop door. He was the epitome of laidback townie. Jared's clock was always set to calm, cool, and collected. Having grown up here, salt water and lazy days were in his blood, balanced with hard work and tenacity.

I walked in the door and studied my friend. I could admit he was a good looking guy. Sun-kissed, strawberry blond hair framed his face in soft waves that brushed the top of his ears. His skin was just as golden as Cole's, just as smooth...hell, his eyes were even blue, although, they didn't hold a candle to—

"Hello?" Jared barked out a laugh. "Why the hell are you lookin' at me like you've never seen me before?"

Scrubbing a hand over my face, the skin beneath burned from getting caught checking him out—or at least trying to. It wasn't the same as when I looked at Cole, and that thought only confused the fuck out of me even more because I'd looked at Cole thousands of times over the last year. Why was it so different now?

"Aiden, what the hell is going on with you?" Jared chuckled, but I could tell I was starting to freak him out.

"Shit. Nothing, sorry. I'm in a weird mood today." Pinching the material of my tee above my chest, I pulled it out a couple of times, trying to cool down my heated skin.

"Uh huh." Jared nodded in a way that said he wasn't buying it. *Yeah, join the fucking club.*

"How did you know you're…?" Shit, was I really about to ask him that? Talk about jumping the fucking gun. Cole and I just started hanging out, if going for one run could be called *hanging out.*

Jared stood up straight, shoving both hands in his pockets. "You're gonna have to give me a little more than that. How did I know I'm…a great dancer? Adorable? Not a mind reader?"

I hung my head and laughed, gripping the back of my neck. "Jesus, I'm losing my damn mind."

Jared joined in the laughter, but then asked, "So, how did I know I'm *what*?"

"Bi."

The simple answer surprised us both. Jared's eyebrows kissed his hairline, his mouth falling open. I flexed my fingers, the palms of my hands sweating so badly I had to wipe them on my running shorts.

"Wow. Okay, that was…huh. Not what I thought you were going to say." He crossed his arms over his chest and studied me like I was a bug under a microscope.

"Forget I asked. It's none of my business. I'm just gonna…" I hiked a thumb over my shoulder toward the shop door and took a step back.

Jared's eyes softened. "I figured it out carefully, at first, but once I'd had my first taste, there was no question in my mind that I wanted more."

"But, what made you…?" Jesus, it was time to grow the hell up and get the words out, because if I couldn't even say it, how was I going to figure it all out? I took a deep breath, then asked, "Was there someone who made you question it?"

"A guy a couple years older than me at my first summer job down at the marina. The boats weren't the only thing I learned how to dock, if ya know what I mean." He wiggled his eyebrows, forcing a laugh from my lips.

"I think I get the gist."

Jared titled his head in thought. "Who's got you questioning?"

"I'm not… There's no one…" I snapped my mouth closed before I embarrassed myself any further. Genuine concern in Jared's eyes loosened the knot that had formed in my chest in a matter of seconds. "I'm not ready to talk about it yet. Fuck, I'm not sure I even want to test the waters, never mind dock the boat. And this…*guy*…" I glanced at Jared, looking for some kind of reaction, but all I saw was my friend giving me his undivided attention. "He's been dicked around—" Wrong choice of words… "He's been hurt before, and the last thing I want to do is drag him into my confusion. I would never fuck with his head, ya know?"

Jared held up his hands in front of him. "Okay. I'm curious as hell, but I'm not gonna push you."

"Thanks, man. Listen, I really do have to go. Gotta pick up my order from my pop's place." I turned to leave, but as I reached the door Jared called out my name.

"I'd say whoever brought you in here, asking that question with that scared as hell look in your eyes, could be worth testing the waters."

I had no idea what to say…because, yeah, Cole was worth so much more than he thought he was…so instead, I nodded.

An hour later, I pulled my van up to Rafferty's back entrance.

I hated wearing my SandBar shirt when I had to see my pop. Hated the way he looked down his nose at me, reminding me how disappointed he was in me and my decision to break from the family business. It was easier to not mention my place, even though that was obviously the reason I was picking up an order to begin with. After going for the run with Cole and then stopping in to see Jared, my morning got away from me. Sure, I could've changed at the bar, but there was a part of me that was tired of acting like that area of my life didn't exist when I was around him. Just once, I wished he'd ask how business was going.

"I don't have all day, Aiden, seein' as how there's no one here to help me." Pop stood in the doorway that led to the backroom, arms crossed over his chest defensively. The years were starting to catch up to him. His once black hair was now completely white, his skin weathered from too many days under the rays before sun damage and sunscreen were considered important. His belly was rounder than it had once been, the lines around his eyes more pronounced from scowling rather than laughing. I knew he was tired, knew he was ready to retire, but the stubborn ass refused to admit it. Billy, Sage's older sister, had expressed interest in the place for years with her husband Scott, but leaving her to run it would mean admitting that Rafferty's was, in fact, staying in the family. It just wasn't going to be run by me.

"You calling me 'no one,' old man?" Billy stuck her head out of the office door with a scowl to match his, giving me a wink before he turned his attention to her. *Note to self: Billy gets bonus fries the next time she's in.*

"Bah...'course not," Pop blustered, his cheeks blotching red. "You're doing what's right, Billy." He flicked hard eyes to me. "Helpin' family, like family should. But, you're taking care of the books. I'm talkin' about helpin' with the day to day."

"You've got two full-time employees; plus, I offered to help with the day to day, and you said—"

"Billy," Pop interrupted, "I think I heard the phone ring. Can you see who it is?"

She narrowed her eyes, hands firmly planted on her hips, knowing she was being dismissed. "I didn't hear the phone." As if he had some hand in it, the phone actually did start to ring. "Saved by the bell"—she pointed a finger at him, raising an eyebrow—"this time, Uncle Jim." Her eyes shifted to me, softening. "Scott and I will see you later, Aiden," she made a point to say, reminding me why I loved my cousin.

"See ya." I stood there in awkward silence with my pop, trying to remember a time when there wasn't animosity between us. My chest ached as my mom's face flashed across my memory. She'd had this way of smoothing out the tension. When she'd died, Pop and I didn't have a buffer any longer. No surprise, a year after that was when I'd taken off for New York.

"Let's get a move on." He waved his hand toward the boxes in the corner. "Those are yours. Packing slip is on the top. You know the drill." He sighed, most likely not even realizing he was rubbing the shoulder that always gave him trouble. "Close the door when you're finished." With that, he turned and headed toward the fermentation room.

Just like Billy had been, I was dismissed.

CHAPTER 5

COLE

Almost two weeks had passed since *Drakegate*, coined by my smartass friends. There were days I didn't know what to do with myself. Fuck the five-second rule; my apartment was so damn clean you could eat off the floor hours later. I'd spent a few mornings with Aiden, running the boards and letting all the thoughts driving me fucking nuts drift off in the ocean breeze. Of course, as soon as I stopped running, those thoughts came back like a fucking boomerang.

Aiden never asked what went down between me and Drake, and I was thankful for it. After the comment I'd made to Aiden about knowing what the hell I was doing when it came to sex, the last thing I wanted to admit was that Drake thought I sucked. Or, rather, the only thing I did well was *suck*.

Then there was the to-do list at my parents' house. The list was already a mile long before my dad threw his back out on the green. Now it was twice as long and he had a sob story about how his second love—golf—betrayed him.

"Sweetie, you know, I saw Jared—from Bait and Switch?—

down at the market. He was buying food for Brutus. He's such a nice young man, don't you think?"

Here we go... "Yup, Jared is really nice, Mom." I reached my hand down as I balanced on the wobbly stool my parents had had since I was a kid. "Scalpel."

She rolled her eyes and handed me the lightbulb. "He told me he's still single."

A sigh rolled out as I screwed the bulb into the light fixture. "He told you or you asked him?"

My mom innocently shrugged her small shoulders. "What difference does it make?"

"Mom, the difference is," I said as I stepped off the stool, "you can't just go around town asking if anyone will date your pathetic son. That's not how it works."

"Don't call my son pathetic. He's just shy and doesn't know his own worth." She nodded with a *hmph*, turning around to resume washing the dinner dishes.

I leaned down and kissed the side of her head, my lips grazing the chestnut hair that was so much like my own. She'd helped it along over the years, giving hers a boost of color to cover up, as she liked to call them, her *wisdom wisps* of gray hair. "Can we stop talking about me in the third person? That would be great. You know what would also be great? If you let *me* worry about my single status."

"You know who else I saw at the market?" she asked, completely ignoring what I just said. "Lynn Myers." She spat the name as if it tasted bad on her tongue. "I never did like that Myers boy. They spoiled him too much."

If I wasn't sure that news had gotten around town about me and Drake, there was my answer.

Dropping down into a chair at the kitchen table, my mom's words faded to the background as Drake's voice infiltrated my calm morning.

You weren't enough.

...fantastic mouth, but the rest leaves something to be desired.

"...she said it like I cared who her sleezy son is dating."

My eyes snapped to her, trying to catch up after tuning her out. "Dating?"

"Haven't you heard a word I said?" She wiped her hands on the blue plaid dish towel in her hands. "Some barely legal clothing designer in Barrett's Port. I had to stand there and listen to her wax poetic about how sweet Drake is to him, and don't get me started on her long and, quite frankly, boring story about the Easter brunch Drake took them all to."

"Them all?" I realized at this point I was just repeating random words my mom was tossing at me, but somewhere between the words *Lynn Myers* and *dating*, my brain had malfunctioned. Because I sure as hell couldn't be hearing this right.

"Yes, his parents and that boy. Are you feeling alright, honey? You look pale." She lifted the back of her soft hand to my brow, then slid it to my cheek. "You don't feel like you have a fever."

"Mom, he brought them all out on *Easter*? A month ago?" I widened my eyes, trying to get her to clue in so I wouldn't have to say it out loud.

"Yes, that's what she...*oh*..." She slumped down into the chair next to me.

"Yeah. *Oh*." A month ago, he'd been fucking me. *A month ago*, he'd said he didn't do relationships. Two weeks ago, he'd said it was just sex, not fairytales and happily-ever-afters. But, one—fucking—month ago, he'd introduced his boyfriend to his parents. The shrimp scampi my mom had made me earlier threatened to make an unwelcome reappearance. I stood up quickly, the chair screeching on the tile floor. "I gotta go."

"Cole..." My mom stood with me, gently grabbing my arm. "Honey..."

I swallowed the lump in my throat. "I'm fine, Mom, I just need to…" What did I need to do? Go home and cry? Pound on Drake's door and ask him what the ever-loving fuck? Drown my sorrows in lager at SandBar? "I need to get my clothes ready for tomorrow." Which was true, but why I'd chosen that as my lame excuse for escape was anyone's guess. I couldn't think straight, and I absolutely hated the pity in my mom's eyes.

I walked to the front door on weak legs. Fresh air was needed if I didn't want to hurl in my parents' house.

"Where are you off to in such a hurry?" my dad asked, fixing his shirt after coming out of the bathroom.

"Not a hurry." *Definitely a hurry.* "Just have some things to get ready for work tomorrow." Raising my hand in goodbye, I gave my mom one last smile, hoping it was enough to wipe the worry from her eyes.

As my feet hit the pavement, I dragged in deep, shaky breaths, flexing and clenching my fingers over and over again. Drake had fucking lied to me. About not wanting a relationship. About sex just being sex. About so many other fucking things. But, the one thing he hadn't lied about was the one thing that hurt the most: I wasn't enough for him, so he'd found someone who was.

My steps felt heavy and aimless. I was such a fucking fool, and the worst part was, the whole town probably knew it. Every person I passed on the sidewalk, every random look I got or wave from a neighbor, made me fucking paranoid. They all had to be thinking that I was a first-class moron, and I couldn't even disagree.

There was no way I could go home, just to beat my head against the wall trying to figure out where I went wrong. My feet ended up taking me to the marina, following the boardwalk in the opposite direction of the inn. The beat of steel drums punctuated every step I took toward SandBar. Shifting my gaze, I looked across the inlet, seeing the lights of the place I'd poured my heart and soul into with four of my closest friends. Four people who would track Drakeula down and introduce his face to the concrete, but that would only serve to draw more attention to my moron status.

So, I followed Jimmy Buffett's voice, telling me it was *five o'clock somewhere.* Hell, I didn't care if it was eight in the freaking morning somewhere; I needed a fucking drink.

SandBar was crowded on Friday nights, but most people took up residence on the outside patio, leaving a few seats open at the bar. I caught the sight of black hair and a strong jawline right before Aiden walked to the other side of the bar.

"Cole!" Sage waved a hand in the air, and I wasn't sure if I was happy or pissed to see my friend. On one hand, I'd come here because I'd needed the distraction, but on the other, something compelled me to come to this particular place—and it wasn't to see Sage.

Reluctantly, I walked over to the empty seat next to him and sat down. "Hey. What are you doing here?"

Sage's dark eyebrows drew together in confusion. Even after working a long day, he looked completely put together. His raven hair was perfectly styled in a short cut, the top swooped back in a wave. He had the faintest tint of mascara on his lashes because he said it made his crystal blue eyes pop. His lips were slightly pink from the lip gloss he loved to wear. Seriously, Levi was blind. "Uh, the same thing you're doing here?"

Not likely. "Right. Sorry. Long day." I glanced around at the crowd, my eyes landing on someone a few seats down the bar from me. Apparently, the universe had a sense of humor tonight. I lifted a hand. "Hey, Jared. How's it goin'?"

"Eh," he replied with a shrug. "Can't complain."

"Really?" Sage chimed in with a skeptical brow. "Because I think it's healthy to find at least one thing to complain about every day. Promotes balance in the body and mind." Sage tapped his temple, a sly smile forming.

"Yeah, that's the reason." The deep voice to our left sent a shiver down my spine. It was one I'd heard too many times to count over the last year, except now, it did strange things to me.

"Listen, dear sweet cousin," Sage began, pointing his fork at Aiden, "you can't have positivity without negativity." He waved his fork in the air. "It throws everything off."

"How so?" Aiden asked, leaning his forearms on the bar. He gave me a wink—that in no way made my belly flip—then flashed his cousin a megawatt smile. "Enlighten me."

Sage set his fork down, brushing his hands together like he was about to school us. He slowly clasped his hands together, setting them down on the bar in front of Aiden. "Think about it. Ignoring negativity creates negativity. Let's say you avoid confrontation, because *ick*...confrontation." He wrinkled his nose, making us all, including Jared, laugh. "But, now you've got this boulder-size weight of unfinished business crushing your chest until you can't breathe. BOOM!" He slammed his hand down on the bar. "Negativity, my friend." He wiggled on his stool, clearly getting into his lecture on the benefits of being negative—which, in and of itself, felt like an oxymoron. "But, let's say you don't let it fester. You get all that shit off your chest, and it's like a weight has been lifted. Positivity." He leaned back in his chair, crossing his arms over his chest with a shit-eating grin. "You've just been *Saged*."

Aiden barked out a laugh, shaking his head at his cousin. "That phrase isn't catching on, no matter how many times you use it."

Sage put his hand up in humorous exasperation, giving Aiden a huff and an eye roll. "Give it time." He sighed, pulling his wallet out of his pocket. "And, with that drop of knowledge, I'm out." He tossed some money down on the gleaming wood of the bar and stood up. "Give Levi a kiss for me," he said to me, his eyebrows wiggling facetiously.

"And, if one of these days I actually *did*, you'd castrate me."

He patted my shoulder blade. "Don't you forget it."

I waved to Sage as he left, turning my gaze back to the bar to find my usual Home of the Wave lager sitting enticingly in front of me. "Thanks," I said to Aiden. There was that flutter again, and believe me, if it was possible to kick myself, I would have.

Aiden studied me for a second. "I think fries are in order." Did he really know me well enough already that he could tell I'd had a shit night and needed comfort food?

"Yep. Extra crispy, extra ranch, please, " I agreed with a resigned sigh. "That obvious, huh?"

Aiden's mouth curled up on one side in a half-smile. "Maybe a little." He tapped the bar in front of me then walked away to take care of my order.

Remembering Jared was there, I chanced a glance his way, seeing if he'd overheard my pitiful plea for potatoes fried to within an inch of their lives and a Jacuzzi of ranch on the side. Luckily, he seemed to be enthralled with something on his phone.

"So," Aiden said, getting my attention again, "ready to talk about it?"

Was I? He'd waited weeks without asking me that question, not that I owed him a response. But something in his kind green eyes—a genuine concern, maybe?—made the thought of telling him a little easier.

Until it was no longer a thought and I opened my damn mouth.

"Drake has a boyfriend. Has *had* a boyfriend for the last month. Some clothing designer from Barrett's Port. Turns out, he's okay with relationships, as long as it's not with me." I was expecting to see more shock in Aiden's eyes. So, when they flickered with sympathy instead, realization hit me square in the chest. "You knew."

"Cole…"

"Fuck, I'm such an idiot." I clumsily got off the stool, sucking in quick breaths. "I need some air."

I vaguely heard Aiden behind me, telling Jesse to cover the bar, but I didn't stop until I was across the patio and my feet hit the sand, taking me close to the water's edge.

"Cole, wait up." Aiden was at my side in seconds, his warm, strong grip around my forearm.

"Why didn't you say anything?" I was angry as hell and taking it out on him. I knew it was a shit move, but fuck if my pride didn't need the shield right now.

"First of all, I didn't know he was his boyfriend. For all I knew, he was just another one of his—" He dropped my arm, leaving my skin cold, and gripped his hips, staring out at the water.

"Another one of his meaningless fucks like me?"

Aiden snapped his head back in my direction. "No! Jesus Christ, Cole. I would never think that about you." He shook his head and dropped his gaze, crossing his arms as he kicked at the sand. "You said all the time you weren't exclusive. That he wasn't doing anything wrong, even though I knew it was a fucking lie and he's a piece of shit. What was the point in bringing it to your attention every time he came in with someone new?"

My anger deflated, my shoulders slumping from the truth of what Aiden had just said. "You're right. I'd told anyone who would listen we weren't exclusive, just to save face when he stood me up. Look where that got me."

"I can sure as fuck guarantee you weren't the only one he cheated on that kid with," Aiden continued. "I say *kid* because he's barely legal drinking age. Hell, I have bottles of rum more mature than he is."

Despite myself, I laughed. Aiden had a way of making me do that lately when I was at my lowest. I turned toward the ocean, shoving my hands in my pockets. "God, I'm such a fool, and I'm sure most of the town knows it. You know how word travels, which is why I don't understand how I didn't hear about this boyfriend sooner. Was I living under a fucking rock?"

"No, you were getting a brand new business on its feet, and gossip isn't your thing. It's not mine either." Aiden gripped my shoulder. "Come on. Your food's probably ready. Don't let that asshole ruin that, too."

"Yeah. Alright." I took a few steps in the direction of the bar but stopped short. "I'm sorry I took that out on you. It's not your fault I couldn't see what was right in front of me." The look in Aiden's eyes was one I couldn't read. Almost like he'd just thought of something, but whatever it was, he kept it to himself.

"Don't worry about it. That's what friends are for."

We walked side-by-side back into the bar, and I sat down on my stool. Seconds later, crispy hot fries were set down in front of me, complete with their ranch bath. Aiden turned around and began clearing a table behind me.

And that's when I heard it.

The voice I wished I could wipe from my mind like a hacker destroys a hard drive. I looked up from my plate, my pulse racing, appetite well and truly blown to smithereens. Sure enough, at a table near Jared, sat Drake and some dark-haired…well…kid. Just like Aiden had said.

"Drakey…if we keep coming here, my ass is going to triple in size." Pouty the Kid pushed his lower lip out, his eyes emulating a puppy's.

Drakey? Had there ever been a more cringe-worthy nickname? Bile rose up in my throat when Drake looked directly at me, a smug smirk lifting the corner of his mouth. As he spoke to

Pouty, he locked eyes with me. "Baby, you know I love your ass. *No one* compares."

Direct hit.

That blatant dig carved out a Drake-sized crater where my heart used to be. For fuck's sake, now was *not* the time for my emotions to betray me, but I could feel the sting of tears line my eyes. To know I wasn't good enough—that I never had been—was a heaping mound of salt on a gaping wound. But, to have it confirmed…to your face…while half the town looked on? My face heated faster than a lit match and my blood pulsed through my veins at a speed that made my head spin and my hands sweat. I glanced around and, sure enough, several eyes were on me. The pity in them made my skin crawl.

"Jared," Drake said, and to Jared's credit, his brows furrowed before he looked back over his shoulder. "Have you met my boyfriend?"

Another grenade tossed, hitting the target of my chest with sickening accuracy.

"Can't say I have," Jared drawled, but for a guy who never lost his cool, there was obvious disgust in his eyes.

"Baby," Drake said, taking Pouty's hand, "come meet Jared." They stood up, walking to Jared's side where Drake still had a clear view of me. "This is Evian Skye, my boyfriend." Because he hadn't said that enough already? "Evian, this is Jared Boone. We went to high school together."

"Evian?" Jared asked, seemingly holding in a laugh. "Like the water?"

Pouty's mouth split with a gleaming-white smile. "Exactly. Water is so soothing, don't you think?" He snaked a hand up Drake's chest, a leer transforming his expression. "Sexy," he said on a dramatic whisper, and I damn near choked on my own spit. Was this guy for real?

"The sexiest man I've ever been with. Had to kiss *a lot* of frogs before I found these lips." Drake bit Pouty's neck with an exaggerated growl.

That grenade missed my heart completely, obliterating my pride instead. I could hear the whispers around me, but when a particular comment of, "*Poor Cole*," came from somewhere behind me, I braced my hands on the bar, ready to push to my feet and make my escape.

"Hey"—a solid, muscular arm slid around my waist and an equally hard body pressed against my side—"my shift's almost over and then we can get the hell out of here." Aiden gripped my side. All I could do was gape at him and open and close my mouth, floundering until he added, in a voice huskier than I'd ever heard from him, "Your place or mine?"

Holy shit, that direct hit landed somewhere else entirely. I shifted in my seat, words escaping me as my pride—and my cock—lit up like fireworks on the Fourth of July. "Huh?" I practically whimpered because I was nothing if not quick on the uptake.

All of my brain cells must have raced to my groin like a magnet, because I could have sworn I heard Jared mutter something about boats docking and, "Now *that's* water worth testing."

CHAPTER 6

AIDEN

I tensed, sliding my gaze over to Jared, and saw the lightbulb moment hit him as mischief sparkled in his eyes. I was never going to live this down, was I? *Your place or mine?* What the hell had I been thinking?

As it was, I had no idea what made me step up and insinuate Cole and I were something we absolutely were *not*. It was the smarter alternative to punching that asshole in the face, though, right? If I thought the murder in Drake's eyes was worth it, it was nothing compared to what I saw in Cole's. When Cole's body relaxed under my hand, his eyes shrinking back to normal size as it dawned on him what my intention was, I could've jumped for fucking joy.

Cole cleared his throat, a slight tremble in his voice. "Um… yours?" he squeaked. For the life of me, I couldn't figure out why that was so adorable. His eyes drifted back over in Drake's direction, a pang of envy hitting me out of nowhere. I followed his gaze, a second rush of pride whooshing over me from the glare Drake was shooting me.

"Since when do you fuck men, Rafferty?" The question was loud, and by the self-satisfied sneer on Drake's face—and the way the bar grew silent—I knew his brazenness had the desired effect. Of course, the way my face burned like fucking lava was also a dead giveaway. A moment ago, the anger coursing through me and the need to protect Cole had clouded my ability to think before I'd opened my mouth. The customers around us—Pointers I'd known all my life—hadn't even been a blip on my radar. Now, the looks I was getting and the whispered questions echoed in my mind. Cole and I both hated gossip, and I'd just made us fodder for the rumor mill for days to come.

"Jesus Christ, Drake. It's none of your damn business," Cole snapped, leaning into my side even more.

The warmth of him, the way he relaxed back into me, as if *I* was the reason he was no longer cowering, quieted the echo until all that was left was my chest once again puffing with satisfaction. *I'd* done that. I'd given Cole a safe place to dock—*that word would never be the same again*—when Drake threatened to drown him in embarrassment and passive-aggressive insults.

I straightened my spine, took a deep breath, pushing all thoughts of *this is a really bad fucking idea* out of my head, and replied, "Since the micro-dick he was getting before me fell a little short." I held my thumb and index finger an inch apart, wincing in sympathy. Cole let out a small sound beside me, burying his laughter in my shoulder. There were gasps and laughs around us as Drake's face turned a comical shade of purple.

"Oh shit," Jared muttered, a snort busting out and a look of *Are you fucking crazy?* on his face. I tried to return the look with what I hoped said, *I know what I'm doing*, but probably came off as, *I've lost my damn mind.*

"Drake, what's going on?" Evian asked, and for a second, I felt bad for the guy. From the look on his face, he truly had no clue.

"Nothing. Let's get out of here." Drake grabbed the smaller man's hand and stormed out.

I scanned the room at all the curious eyes on me. "Okay, people. Show's over." Cole swiveled on the stool until he faced me.

"Uh, Aiden, can I talk to you in private?" He didn't wait for my response, grabbing my hand as he hopped down off the stool and dragged me back toward my office. A chorus of catcalls erupted behind us.

Cole closed us in the small space, hands on his hips, staring at me so hard I looked away. "What the hell were you thinking?"

That got my back up. It was a good thing my office was in the back and the loud music would drown us out. "Do you really give a shit if that asshole thinks you're taken?" Damn, when was he going to learn—

"No. I give a shit that half the town thinks you and I are together, and by tomorrow morning the rest of the town will know! Because you're *straight*, Aiden! Or have you forgotten? You should give a shit because now people think we're fucking." I flinched from that one word. "So, I repeat, what were you thinking?"

Gripping my hair, I paced in front of the door. "I wasn't thinking, okay? He was digging into you, and you weren't saying anything! It was like you were frozen." I stopped short and faced him. "You don't know how close I came to hitting that bastard."

That seemed to knock Cole's temper down a peg or two. "Why? I mean, don't get me wrong, I'm grateful. He…was *really* determined to prove I'm nothing more than dirt on the bottom of his shoe. I mean, did all of Coral Pointe really need to know that I'm not…?" Cole didn't finish whatever he was about to say and slumped down into the chair in front of my desk with a huff. "The last thing I wanted to do was pull you into that shitshow."

I moved in front of him, sitting down on the hard wood of the desk. "You didn't pull me in, I jumped…admittedly, without a net or a plan." Exhaling, I scrubbed a hand over my face, the day and my brilliant public declaration sitting like a thirty-pound weight on my shoulders. No doubt, the news would reach Sage before the night was over. The rest of my family would find out by tomorrow. I knew my cousins wouldn't give a shit who the hell I was with, but lying to them? That was another issue. I clearly hadn't thought this through. Didn't matter. It was out in the wild now. "Wait…Coral Pointe doesn't need to know that you're not what?"

Pink flooded his cheeks as he averted his eyes. "Nothing. Forget I said anything." He rubbed his palms on his thighs, his gaze flicking to me and then away again. There was something he wasn't telling me, but I wasn't going to push him. "Look, it doesn't matter anyway. It'll be obvious by tomorrow that it's not true. We can just laugh it off as a joke."

Something about that didn't sit right with me. "And what about Drake?"

Cole dropped his gaze and shrugged. "Doesn't matter."

Except it *did* matter. I'd thrown this out there, and now Cole had to deal with the aftermath. Jesus, I was an idiot.

I studied Cole's despondent expression, the way his brows came together in worry. He bit his bottom lip—his *plump* bottom lip—and there was that foreign feeling again in the pit of my stomach. I took in the way his navy blue tee clung to his chest, how the golden tan of his legs stretched out in front of him. I couldn't see his eyes, but I knew they'd pop against the chestnut color of his hair and his tanned face.

We'd been running together a few times a week, and his long lean muscles were evidence of that. Come to think of it, I'd seen Cole more in the last few weeks than I had since he'd moved back. Hell, we were already spending time together between our morning runs and when he came to the bar. We didn't have to be into public displays of affection for people to believe we were together. We could basically just keep doing what we were already doing.

"No."

Cole's eyes jerked up, confusion morphing his expression. "No? No *what*?"

"Let's just go along with it." I held my hands up in front of me when Cole opened his mouth to argue. "No, hear me out. We can still hang out like we've been doing…going for runs and whatnot." I wasn't sure what the *whatnot* meant since we hadn't done much more than run together and see each other here at the bar. "In a few weeks, we can amicably stop seeing each other, and continue with business as usual."

"Business as usual?"

I blew out a breath. "You know what I mean. After a few weeks, Drake will be out of your system. Like detox." Cole snorted making me chuckle at how ridiculous this was all sounding, but the plan had merit. "He'll be out of your life, we get to keep our friendship, and no one will be the wiser."

Cole sat up in the chair, shaking his head. "I don't know, Aiden. You shouldn't have to do this just because I'm a weak asshole with no willpower. This is your life, too. Don't you care what people will think?"

"I think most people won't give a shit, some people will know it's not true but keep their mouths shut, and everyone else already looks down their noses at me because they think I betrayed my family." I rolled my eyes, so sick of that last one. A laugh bubbled out. "Having my sexuality be the topic of gossip instead of what a shit son I am will be a welcome change."

A smile finally split Cole's pink lips as he huffed out a laugh. "You're really okay with this? Because it's okay if you're not, but…I don't know… Maybe if we do this it'll give me time to just"—he quirked a half-smile—"detox, I guess? Like you said. Sounds so pathetic when I say it out loud."

I kicked the side of his foot so he'd look at me. "It's not stupid that you give a shit. That's the difference between you and Drake. He *is* toxic, and you don't need that in your life."

Cole slapped his hands on his thighs then stood up. "Well, I guess I should… I should probably get going. I think I'm done with peopling for the day." He dug in his pocket and pulled out his wallet.

"Don't worry about the tab. It's on me, *boyfriend*." I snorted and scrunched my nose. "That sounded weird."

Cole's laugh bounced off the four walls of my small office. "Maybe if you didn't put so much emphasis on the word it wouldn't. Or, you know, just use my name."

"Yeah, I suppose so." I smiled as I stood up, losing my breath for a second when I realized how close we were standing. So close I could feel the heat coming off his body and smell the woodsy cologne that was becoming familiar to me. I swallowed hard. Whatever this was…this reaction I was having toward Cole lately…I needed to figure it the fuck out. The sound of a text coming through cut through the silence in the room, and I fished my phone out of my pocket. "Uh oh…"

"What?"

"A text from Sage, and I quote, 'What the actual fuck?' Jeez, that didn't take long, huh?"

"You sure you're ready for this?"

I waved a hand in the air. "*Pfft*, yeah. Piece of cake." I was not fucking ready. I was nowhere near ready, but I'd signed up for this and dragged Cole down with me, so I was going to see it through.

Cole gave me a side-eyed glance. "Okay. If you're sure…"

"I'm sure."

He looked at me skeptically, but when my phone rang in my hand, he nodded once and took a step toward the door, stopping short of opening it. "Oh, wait…people expect us to leave together now." A blush tinged his cheeks. Why that was so adorable, I had no idea—but it so fucking was.

"Right. Okay, I'm just gonna answer Sage before he gets pissed and comes back here. Can you hang out a bit longer?"

"Yeah, I'll be at the bar." He let himself out, closing the door behind him.

Taking a deep breath, I answered the phone. "Miss me already? You were just here, cuz."

"Don't you *cuz* me, Aiden Rafferty. What the hell were you thinking?"

"So, we're just jumping right into it then? No pretenses or small talk?"

"Aiden…" Sage warned.

I blew out another long breath and sank down into my office chair. "It's not a big deal."

"Not a big deal? Do you even hear yourself? You outed yourself tonight…in front a bar full of people… And, oh, let's not forget the most important part… You're straight, Aiden!"

"What I did was help a friend. You weren't here, Sage. You didn't hear the way Drake was embarrassing him. Cole deserves so much better than that. All he needs is a few Drake-free weeks to realize he's ten times better than that asshole and Drake's new boy toy combined. I don't even know what the hell Drake sees in that kid. He had a great man in Cole, and he threw it all away for—"

"Holy shit," Sage said, stopping me mid-sentence.

"What?"

"You like him."

"What? Of course I like Cole. What the hell do you mean?"

"No, you *like him* like him."

My heartbeat surged into overtime. "Sage, don't make this something it's not."

Sage's laugh came through the speaker. "Oh, I don't need to.

You did that all on your own, cuz. Question is, why?"

I didn't really have a logical answer for that. Logic hadn't played a part in claiming Cole and I were a thing. Hell, logic had taken a seat, put its feet up, grabbed some popcorn, and watched me jump into that lie while taking Cole down with me. "Honestly? I really don't know. It just…came out."

Sage sighed. "So did you, apparently. What are you gonna do when people find out it's not true?"

I leaned my elbow on my desk, my hand cradling my head. "Funny story…"

"Oh no…"

"You see, I decided maybe it's for the best…"

"Don't say it…"

"…if Cole and I keep up the charade for a few weeks."

"You said it. You *actually* said it." Sage started muttering under his breath about stupid cousins and stupid friends and testosterone-fueled, whose-dick-is-bigger spitting contests. He wasn't wrong. "Someone's gonna get hurt. You know that, right?"

I sat up ramrod straight, my hackles rising. "I would never hurt Cole."

"Not intentionally."

"Sage," I said, exhaustion sinking into my bones, "I've worked a long day, I'm tired… Can we talk about this tomorrow? I promise you can yell at me all you want."

"I'm not going to yell at you," he softly said. I grunted my disbelief. "Okay, I'm not going to yell at you *again*. What you did for Cole was really sweet, Aiden. I just hope you realize what you're getting yourself into. I don't want to see either one of you get hurt."

"We won't. I promise. I'll talk to you tomorrow."

But, even after I'd made the promise and hung up, there was a part of me that wasn't so sure one of us wouldn't get hurt—and another part of me that was worried which one of us it would be.

CHAPTER 7

COLE

I managed to make it to the inn without running into any nosy neighbors or even getting a call from my mom. I wasn't sure whether to be happy about that last one or worried. Silence from Helen Sullivan was rarely a good thing.

I loved the inn at this hour of the morning, so calm and peaceful—except for the clanging and voices usually coming from the kitchen. Most pronounced was always Burke's.

So, the unsettling quiet coming from the room was unexpected to say the least. I peeked my head in, looking for the larger man among his employees, but his big head was nowhere to be found. "Where's Burke?" I asked Megan, Burke's sous chef.

"Hey, Cole," she replied with a teasing grin. *Fuck, she must know.* She narrowed her eyes and put a finger to her chin. "Hmmm…you look different this morning. New haircut?" Yep, she knew. "New shirt?"

"Yeah, yeah. Get it all out now." I rolled my eyes and chuckled.

"Oh! Wait, I know! New *man*?" She wiggled her eyebrows.

"Had no idea Aiden Rafferty swung both ways." She sighed dramatically, the back of her hand pressed to her forehead. "The entire single population of Coral Pointe is in mourning today."

"Cute. Are you done?"

She thought about it for a second, a finger to her chin. "I think so."

"Great. Now can you tell me where Burke is?"

She shook her head, mock sympathy on her face. "I'm afraid I can't."

"What? Why not?"

"Because where's the fun in that?" An evil grin morphed her otherwise pretty face.

I banged my head against the doorframe. "Remind me to address your smartass sass in your review."

"*Pffft*…you could, but you and I both know I'm the only buffer you have between Mr. Grumpy Pants and the rest of the kitchen staff, soooo…" She rapidly blinked her eyes, feigning innocence she was nowhere near possessing.

"I hate you," I grumbled, a smile forming even though I knew it was a mistake to humor her.

Turning to walk away, I heard her call out, "You love me and you know it!"

One of the best decisions we'd ever made was hiring Megan Lanter. She was a born and raised Pointer, just like me. She'd graduated a year ahead of me with Drake and Jared, and had no problem expressing her fondness for one man and not the other. Anyone could figure out which one she hated with a passion—even the man himself. Somehow, she took Burke's moods with a grain of salt and a dash of sarcasm thrown right back at him. It was a blast to watch.

On the way to my office, I decided if I was going to have to deal with shit today, I needed to be caffeinated. Stopping in the breakroom, I filled my favorite mug to the rim, the aroma from the dark liquid awakening my senses. I meandered down the hall to my and Levi's office and froze in the entryway like a teenager caught sneaking in after curfew. Burke faced the door, arms crossed over his chest, his eyes narrowed from the scowl directed at me. Levi turned his chair, an equally scrutinizing expression in his eyes.

"Oh, for fuck's sake. Quit it with the looks, Mom and Dad." I huffed, dropping my lunch bag down on my desk. "Too bad Noah and Ford aren't here to join in the interrogation."

Burke and Levi held up their phones simultaneously, Ford's goofy grin on one screen and Noah's on the other. I wished my two happy-go-lucky friends were actually here. Instead, I was stuck waiting to be lectured by Grumpy and Grumpier. Noah and Ford were the balance in this crazy group, rarely letting anything get to them, while Burke and Levi had perfected their scowls. And then there was me, somewhere in the middle.

"Why did we have to hear from Teresa down at Beachin' Bakery that you're, and I quote, 'shacking up with that hunky Rafferty boy?'" Burke asked, a line pinched between his brows.

"Yeah, he is," Ford chimed in with a beaming smile, sounding like a proud parent. "You *get* ya some, Cole. Aiden's got an ass you could eat off of. Have you done that yet?"

Coffee spewed out of my mouth and nose, the brown liquid landing on my desk and some on Levi's. Grabbing several tissues from the box, I mopped up the mess I'd made.

"Ford, focus," Burke snapped, a sly smile breaking through.

"Dammit, you know I hate it when you say that. I'm not a fucking car, dude, and if I were, I'd be a Ferrari with the way my engine revs." He bit his bottom lip and made some movement with his hand that was probably supposed to come off as lewd but, on the small phone screen, looked like he was a kid trying to get an eighteen wheeler to honk its horn.

I leaned back in my chair, linking my hands together as I

rested them on my stomach. "Yeah, I'm not sure speed is something you want to brag about in regards to sex, unless you're okay admitting you finish first."

"Hey, I'll have you know, my stamina is fucking fine, thank you. Better than fine. It's the stuff of legends. As a matter of fact, I'll be showcasing my stamina tonight."

"Can we move off the topic of Ford's sex life, please," Levi groused, looking uncomfortable all of a sudden.

I laughed. "Why? So we can move on to the topic of mine?"

"Exactly," Noah said. "Give us the deets. Last I checked, Aiden was straight. Hot as hell, but still straight."

I blew out an exasperated breath. "Drake was in the bar last night with his new boyfriend." It was almost funny watching their angry and amused faces transform to disgust.

"Since when does he have a boyfriend?" The question came from Levi this time, his fingers drumming on the desk the way they always did when he was trying to rein in his anger.

"Oh, did I forget to mention he started seeing him over a month ago?"

"That son of a bitch," Burke snapped.

"Wait, what does that have to do with you and Aiden?" Noah asked, bringing us back around to the whole point of the Office Inquisition.

"Drake was kind of making a scene. You know, flexing his muscles by way of indirect insults." I dropped my eyes, the embarrassment resurfacing again, heat flooding my cheeks. "Except, everyone knew they were aimed at me and how inferior my *skills* are compared to Pouty the Kid."

Ford's laugh boomed through the phone. "Pouty the Kid."

"I still don't see what this has to do with Aiden." Leave it up to Levi to push for more info. That was until the lightbulb moment clearly flashed in his eyes. "You told Drake you're with Aiden?"

Okay, maybe that lightbulb was the wrong wattage.

"No! I would never do that." I groaned, hanging my head back as I looked to the ceiling. "Aiden put his arm around my waist, pretended we were a thing, and insinuated we were leaving together." I dropped my chin to look at them. "As in, *leaving* together. Then, Drake blatantly—without an ounce of class or tact, I might add—asked Aiden in front of the whole bar when Aiden started fucking guys."

All four jaws dropped with that little tidbit of information.

"Man, why do we miss all the good stuff," Ford grumbled. "What did Aiden say?"

I pictured the only part of last night that I still couldn't believe happened, and smiled. "He basically implied that Drake has a small dick, and he could give me *more*." I squirmed in my chair. Even talking about Aiden's dick, as if it was something I had access to, sent a jolt straight to mine. "I'd never seen Drake that mad. He grabbed Pouty's hand and dragged him out of there so fast."

"*Damn*…Aiden just got ten degrees hotter." Noah fanned himself.

Yeah, no shit.

That had been my fucking problem ever since last night. I couldn't get his words out of my head. *Since the micro-dick he was getting before me*… Before me, as in, he was the one fucking me now. Jesus Christ, I tried to push the thought out of my head, truly I did, but it was no use. My mind latched onto that claim and ran with it, not to mention what my hand did remembering those words while in bed last night. Made the thought of seeing him again a wee bit awkward. But who could fucking blame me? He'd thrown that visual out there for everyone to make of it what they would. My mind chose to make it a group of vivid, lurid images, replaying over and over again until I'd had no choice but to quiet them.

When the guys stared at me, waiting for me to make sense of all this, I broke down and told them about Aiden's idea to keep the charade going for a few weeks. Of course, Ford and Noah said they were completely onboard before they both got off the calls, and Levi didn't hesitate to make it known he thought it was a bad idea.

Burke gripped my shoulder on the way out. "I better not hear secondhand shit around town anymore. Keep us updated, wouldya?" When I nodded sheepishly, he added, "And if you happen to take part in that meal, I better fucking hear about it. You know taste is my favorite of all the senses." He walked out of the office, leaving me confused and trying to figure out what the hell he was talking about. I replayed the convo, my face flaming and my dick filling as Ford's question popped into my mind. *Aiden's got an ass you could eat off of. Have you done that yet?*

"There will be no tasting!" I yelled, Burke's booming laughter echoing down the hallway.

Rolling my eyes, I exhaled long and slow and turned back to my desk, caught by the unreadable look in Levi's eyes.

"Just say it, Levi, whatever it is." I stiffened my spine, preparing for a one-on-one reprimand, but something in Levi's stare made me soften the scowl I was giving him.

"Unrequited love is a bitch, Cole. You already went through that with Drake. Just…be careful. Don't make this fake…whatever the hell it is…something it's not. At the end of the day, Aiden's still straight, and technically, you're still single." The pain in Levi's eyes was staggering. Had he been through something similar? We normally told each other everything, but I knew Levi. He'd tell us when he was ready.

Nodding, I pushed up from my chair and moved my lunch bag to the filing cabinet behind me. "I have to go check on Miss Margie." I got to the door, stopping abruptly. I couldn't let that line about unrequited love hang in the air. He wasn't going to talk until he was ready, but at least I could remind him… "We're here, you know. If you ever need to talk."

He sucked in a breath, his eyes popping for a fraction of a second before he schooled his features. Finally, he cleared his throat and said, "I'm fine, Cole."

"Just…keep it in mind."

He pressed his lips together and nodded, turning his attention back to the Excel spreadsheet on his computer screen.

My phone rang and I pulled it out, groaning when I saw who was calling me. "Hi, Mom." I made my way down the hall, bracing myself for what was coming next.

"You know, the strangest thing happened today…" *Here we go…* "I was standing in line at the post office with Aunt Carrie's birthday gift, minding my own business, as I do." I rolled my lips in for that one, stifling a laugh. "In walks Irma, and she has the nerve to ask me when my son started seeing Aiden Rafferty." *Shit.* "Of course, I only have one son, whom I just saw last night, and assured her she must have heard wrong."

"Mom…"

"Well, wouldn't you know, in chimes Edna Lawry, my beloved, crotchety neighbor—wearing green, I might add, which is definitely *not* her color." She couldn't resist a dig at good ol' Edna. "And Edna claims her nephew—you know, the one who broke my kitchen window with a baseball?"

"He was nine, Mom." Jeez, my mom was never going to forgive the poor guy.

"He said he was in the bar last night when Aiden…you know, your *boyfriend*…pointed out Drake's"—she cleared her throat—"shortcomings, and then kissed you, right there in the middle of SandBar, for everyone to see."

That guy always was a little shit.

"That's not true," I argued because I sure as hell would have remembered if Aiden had planted a big one on me right there in front of the draft beer. But when she sighed her relief into the phone, I added, "Well, not all of it is true."

"Cole David Sullivan, is it true or is it not? Because I just met a handsome man at the doctor's office this morning and bragged all about my single, gay son."

I was grateful for her support. Both my parents had been amazing when I came out, but holy hell, she was out of control with trying to set me up lately. "Mom, how do you know he's even gay? And please don't tell me you asked him."

"Of course not!" she said incredulously. "I asked Norma at the front desk."

Halting in the hallway, I groaned, switching directions to head out onto the back patio. "Oh my god. You have to stop doing that."

"Well, honey, I wouldn't have done it had I known you're seeing someone. Aiden Rafferty, of all people."

"What's wrong with Aiden?" I hadn't meant for the question to come out so defensive, but I gripped the phone, holding in an apology for the anger in my voice. There was nothing wrong with Aiden. He was a smart businessman, kind to anyone he met, and sexy as hell. And he was incredibly protective of his friends, given what he'd done for me the night before.

"There's nothing wrong with Aiden, honey. Calm down." The softening of her voice loosened my shoulders that were stiff with tension. "I just meant it was unexpected. I've only known Aiden to date women. Plus, it seemed like you weren't over Drake yet."

I rubbed my hand over my chest, still feeling the ache of how Drake so thoroughly made it known I'd meant nothing to him. The thing was, though, something Levi had just said to me really didn't sit right. Yeah, Drake broke my heart and used me, but was I actually in love with him? Was this what unrequited love felt like?

"You really like Aiden, though, don't you?"

Yeah. Yeah, I really did. "Of course I like him. He's a great guy." Technically, it wasn't a lie.

"Why didn't you tell me last night? I was so worried when you left."

I was caught between a rock and a hard place. That was exactly what I'd done last night, but not because Aiden was *actually* my boyfriend. God love my mom, but she thrived on gossip with the best of them. I was waiting for the day she joined the Walkie Talkies. Maybe that's where my aversion to gossip came from. My mom did enough gossiping for the whole family. Even with her best efforts, she'd slip and tell someone that Aiden and I weren't really together. I wasn't ready for that cat to be out of the bag. Drake would be all over it, and instead of him using how bad I was in the sheets, he'd have a field day throwing my pathetic need to hide behind a fake boyfriend in my face.

I hated that Aiden was taking the brunt of this, though. His sexuality was the topic of the day, just like I thought it would be. How was he okay with this?

"Mom, things between me and Aiden are new." *Really fucking new.* "We had a feeling people would make a big deal out of it." Also not a lie. "Can you just, for once, believe me when I tell you I'm okay?" Which was oddly…kind of true.

She sighed with a low hum. "Okay. I'll take your word for it. That being said, when are you and Aiden coming over for dinner?"

"It's hard with our schedules to coordinate a night where one of us isn't working." Man, I was getting good at saying the truth without saying the truth.

"Make time, Cole," she said in the no-nonsense tone she'd perfected. "Oh! I almost forgot. I'm on the Memorial Day Festival Committee again this year." Like she'd been every year since I was ten. I cringed, dreading what was coming next. "Let me know what you want to volunteer for. You know, it's only a week away."

"Mom, I just told you, I'm really busy. The inn is completely booked and we're having a food tent at the festival. Plus, Shore Thing Tours will be holding signups for summer activities. We all need to help out."

"All of you…meaning all five of you, plus your employees? I think you can spare an hour or two helping someplace else, don't you think? For me?"

My mom was as good at guilt trips as she was at gossiping.

"Fine. Send me the list and I'll go over it. But it can only be for a couple of hours, Mom."

"Sure, honey."

"I'm serious."

"Uh huh. Got it."

Oh, she got it alright. Question was, would she actually listen? "Mom, I have to go."

"Okay. I love you."

"Love you, too."

The call ended, and I found Aiden's name in my phone. I started writing a text, but hell…he was my boyfriend, after all, right? I hit send on my phone, listening as it rang. After the fifth ring, I was about to end the call when I heard Aiden's deep voice say hello.

"Uh, hey." I felt stupid now. We'd never talked on the phone.

"Hey." It sounded like he held a hand over the receiver when I heard a muffled, "Table ten still hasn't gotten their jalapeno poppers and twelve needs menus." There was a brushing sound in my ear then, "Sorry about that."

"Busy?"

He laughed. "You could say that. You'd think people in this town have never been here before. We haven't been this busy on a

Sunday in…probably ever. Hell, I'm not even supposed to be working today, but Jesse called me in a panic."

"That's good, right?"

"Well, if the customers were actually here for the food, I'd say yes, but it seems I'm Coral Pointe's main attraction today."

"Shit. Aiden, I'm so sorry."

"What are you sorry for? I knew what I was getting myself into…sort of."

"Well, I guess that answers my question. I was calling to see how you were holding up. I've already been interrogated by the guys and given the VIP treatment in guilt trips by my mom."

"You say 'holding up' like someone died, Cole. It's a bunch of gossip. We'll only be exciting until something more interesting comes along." There was another shuffle. "Besides, is it so terrible that people think we're together and are showing their support?" He'd lowered the volume of his voice, making that question sound huskier as it vibrated against my ear. A shiver raced down my spine.

Was it? I mean, it could be worse, right? "No, of course not. I just know you're taking the brunt of it."

"I'm good. It's not the first time I've been the topic of conversation around here. At least this time it's on a positive note, for the most part." He played it off like a joke, but it wasn't hard to hear the underlying pain. A lot of people, mainly older Pointers, were loyal to Jim Rafferty to a fault. As if Aiden had actually betrayed his father and his family. It was ridiculous.

"Aiden…" I struggled with what to say, so I went with, "I may not be a bartender, but I have two functioning ears and thirty-three years' worth of patience I've built up from being my mother's son. If you ever need to vent, I'm here."

There was a long pause on the other end of the phone before he finally said, "I know you are." Those four words, his trust in me, lit up inside me. Why I was so proud to be someone he trusted was beyond me. The only thing I knew was I wanted to keep it that way. Our friendship would never be the same after all this was over, but maybe it could be stronger. "Listen, I have to go," he said, "but thanks for calling to check on me. See, we're doing this boyfriend thing well, don't you think?"

"It still sounds weird when you say it."

Aiden laughed into the phone. "I'll talk to you later."

I turned around, catching my reflection—and the enormous grin on my face—in the window of the French door. If someone had asked me in the midst of my humiliation last night if I would be this happy today, I would have laughed—or possibly cried—in their face. But, there it was. The proof, right in front of me. I just never would've guessed that Aiden would be the reason.

CHAPTER 8

AIDEN

Three days after *Drakemegeddon*, the bar was still busy as hell. I felt like I'd been run over by the Walkie Talkies as I let myself in my house. Who the hell knew my love life would be so damn interesting to the people of Coral Pointe? If only they knew that my love life was actually as real as the Easter Bunny.

I'd forgotten what it was like to be in a relationship. I missed holding hands with someone, or being thought of as the other half of a whole. I had the latter now, under false pretenses. The former—along with dating and laughing and sex, for fuck's sake—was still something I longed for. Three years of being a bachelor, and suddenly I was part of a *couple*. You know what was worse than friends with benefits? Boyfriend with no benefits.

I hadn't seen Cole since the infamous night of my *coming out*. There was a part of me that felt guilty for the lie, and another part of me that wondered if it was a lie at all. It didn't feel like a lie as I set the bag of takeout from Tuscany by the Sea on the counter then dragged my exhausted ass into the shower. The nervous knots didn't feel like a lie, either. Or the way I put on cologne, even though we weren't going anywhere.

Glancing at the clock on my phone, I took advantage of the ten minutes I still had before Cole would be here and pulled up Jared's name.

Jared picked up on the second ring. I breathed a sigh of relief until I heard his easy-going chuckle. "Freaking out already?"

"No, I'm not freaking out. Why the hell do I tell you anything in the first place? Don't answer that." Jared was full-on laughing. "It's just part of the façade, right? I mean, who's gonna believe we're together if we never spend time together, right? He doesn't have to know I've been confused lately, right? I just said *right* three times, didn't I?"

"Sure did. Take a few deep breaths, man. You're making *me* anxious."

"Sorry." I slumped down onto the couch, leaning my head back on the cushion.

"Aiden, this doesn't have to be complicated. Spend some time with the guy. Let things happen naturally. If anything, you'll get closer as friends." I'd been nervous going to Jared for advice, but I was so grateful for it now. This didn't feel like something I could figure out on my own. If anyone could talk a guy off a ledge, it was Jared. Except I wasn't so sure which direction I wanted to go. Back to my old life, working too much as it passed me by? Or forward, into something terrifyingly new but exciting in a way nothing had ever been before?

"Yeah, you're right. I—" My doorbell rang and there went my racing pulse again. "He's here. I gotta go."

"Cool. Let me know how it goes."

I ended the call, took a deep breath, then walked to my front door and opened it. There were those nervous knots again. The sun was going down, casting a soft glow of purple and pink behind him. He was holding a six pack, the dusting of dark hair on his forearms catching the light—something I'd never noticed about a guy before. Who the hell looked at arm hair? Me, apparently.

"Um…can I come in?" A flicker of doubt crossed his face.

"Yes. Of course. Sorry." I moved out of his way, breathing in his cologne as he breezed past me. It wasn't unusual to like another guy's cologne, right? *There you go again.*

About to swing the door shut, I caught a glimpse of Teresa across the street, pulling her curtain back. I waved at her, letting her know that… *yeah, I see you and I know what you're up to.* No doubt, Cole and I would be the talk of the bakery tomorrow morning. She waved back sheepishly and let the curtain slide closed. I shut the door and turned to find Cole standing there, an uneasiness in his stance.

"Teresa?"

"Yep," I replied on a sigh, taking a couple of steps closer. "Too bad we didn't give her a real show, huh?"

A shy smile curled Cole's mouth as he looked down at his feet. "Could you imagine?"

Yeah, I can…more and more these days. I kept that thought to myself and snorted, opting for humor instead. "I'm pretty sure she was."

Cole's head popped up and a laugh bubbled out. "Gross." His eyes immediately widened, his hand flying up in front of him. "Not that kissing you would be gross…at all. No doubt you're a great kisser. I just meant I don't want creepers to watch us kiss—hypothetically! Not like *kissing* kissing. Oh my god, I'll shut up now." He covered his eyes, his cheeks flushing that shade of pink that was completely…adorable.

I couldn't help but laugh as I took the last step toward him and pulled his hand away from his face. "I knew what you meant." There was a heartbeat…two…where we just stared at one another. Seconds where I took in what I could of his ocean blue eyes and the light dusting of freckles across his nose. I'd never noticed them before.

Cole cleared his throat nervously, his eyes shifting down. I was still holding his hand. This was the second time I'd done that. The only reason I could come up with for why I did it was it felt *right* there…in mine. But I'd be damned if my confusing thoughts made Cole uncomfortable in any way. So, I let his hand go and crossed my arms, rocking back on my heels.

"So…" Cole said then hiked a thumb over his shoulder. "I can put this beer in your fridge. D-do you want to eat?"

"Right. Food!" My enthusiasm over carbonara and ravioli broke the tense barrier between us.

Cole nodded once. "Food."

Filling our plates, we each grabbed a beer and walked with into the living room. I wasn't big on formal dining. Besides, this night was already proving to be awkward enough without the added pressure. I reminded myself again that this was Cole. If nothing else, he was my friend. The same guy I'd run with for the last few weeks, and who liked my Home of the Wave lager so much, he'd brought some to have with dinner. The same guy who ordered extra crispy French fries every time he was upset and key lime pie when he was happy. I'd brought some of that home, too.

We sat on the couch in silence at first, settling into a situation we'd never been in before. I found myself caught up in the way he carefully twirled his fork in the long pasta, gathering bacon and creamy sauce to make the perfect bite. He lifted the fork to his mouth, sliding the food off onto his tongue before licking his pink lips. I nearly swallowed my tongue as I watched his strong jaw move, his Adam's apple lift as he swallowed. It was safe to say, I was attracted to him. Possibly more than I'd thought.

"You're not eating."

"What?" I looked down at my untouched ravioli. "Oh, right." *Right? For the love of...* My eyes fell once more of their own volition to his bottom lip. When his tongue snaked out again, I envisioned it doing more than just cleaning the white sauce from his mouth. *Holy shit.* I cleared my throat, quickly looking away. "Did I mention I'm exhausted? The bar's been crazy. It wasn't a great day in general."

"We don't have to do this tonight." His brows furrowed and he leaned forward, setting his plate down on the coffee table.

"No, I want you here." Grabbing his forearm, I stopped him before he could stand up. His skin was warm beneath my hand. The hair I'd noticed before, coarse to the touch on the top of his forearm in juxtaposition with the smooth skin on the bottom. I found myself brushing my thumb back and forth over that smooth skin. It took me a second to realize he was giving me a strange look. I replayed my words back through my head, internally cursing myself when it hit me. "I mean, you don't need to go. I like the company." I let go of his arm and softly laughed. "Guess I'm never satisfied. There are too many people at work, and not enough people here."

His shoulders relaxed, the leg nearest to me bending in front of him and sliding onto the couch, his knee against the back cushion as he faced me. I tried to ignore the way his shin pressed up against the length of my thigh. "I know exactly what you mean. Today was the day from hell. First one of the washing machines broke, then a guest complained they didn't have enough towels and we didn't have any to give them right then because, *hello*, broken washing machine. Then a kid was jumping on the furniture in the lobby, even though I'd asked, politely, several times for him to stop. His damn parents, of course, said nothing, until the kid fell and hit his head on the tile—no blood thank god. Then all of a sudden it was my fault. His mom freaked the hell out, but thank god the dad had some common sense, finally telling the kid that was what he got for not listening." He leaned toward the coffee table and picked up his beer, taking a swig before continuing. "To top it all off, my mom called and said I took too long to get back to her on what I'd volunteer for at the festival, so she signed me up for something."

"Oh shit."

"Yeah, oh shit. And here's the kicker… She won't tell me what it is!" Cole genuinely laughed, his beaming smile lighting up his whole face, his blue eyes dancing with humor. Shaking his head he sighed and said, "You'd think after all that, I'd want some peace and quiet at home. Problem is, it's too quiet."

"Yeah, I get it. Don't get me wrong, I'll never be upset that the bar is busy, but I swear, some of those people are waiting for you to come in. As if we'd make out right there for their entertainment."

"Think we could sell tickets? Might be worth it. Washing machines don't fix themselves, you know." Cole wiggled his eyebrows, the laid-back person I'd come to expect from him when he was with the guys shining through. Something about that…the way he relaxed enough for me to see a glimpse of *that* Cole…made me feel weightless. The stress from the day melted away in the heat pooling in my groin. *Rein it in, Aiden.*

"Wait, I thought you said Teresa watching us kiss would be gross?" How many times could two people reference kissing one another in one night without *actually* doing it?

"Well, yeah…because we're here, at your home, and deserve some privacy. Kissing in public is just asking for an audience." Cole shrugged. "Might as well get something out of it."

"Noted," I replied, not bothering to hide the promise in the word. I wasn't counting anything out at this point. Cole stared at me, as if trying to decipher if I meant what he thought I did. At least, that's how I read his expression.

"Um…so was there anything else that happened today? You said it wasn't so great." He set his beer down and picked up his pasta again, eyes locking on mine while he took another bite.

Remembering that morning, I put my ravioli down and picked up my beer for a long swallow. "Same as every other time I stop in to see my pop, I guess. He won't let me help with any repairs, but then goes on and on about family and how they should be there for each other. I don't get how he can insinuate I'm not there for my family while simultaneously refusing any help I try to give. Billy is ready to knock the old man out. I don't know how many times she has to tell him she's ready and willing to take over." I laughed humorously. "Of course, if she did take over, what would my pop have to hold over my head?"

Cole nodded his understanding. "Ah…parents are so good at guilt trips, aren't they? Like, is there a class or something?"

"There has to be because he's damn good at it. Award-winning good at it. He barely has to use words anymore to make me feel like shit. It's impressive." I set my beer back down, my stomach roiling, deciding to just go for complete transparency. "When my mom got sick, I'd stepped up more at Rafferty's. He was with her a lot, and I was…well, I was avoiding the inevitable. She was our rock. She was what held us together."

Cole rested his elbow on the back of the couch, still facing me, his rapt attention compelling me to shift toward him. We were like two bookends facing each other. I mirrored his position, shin pressing against his, my fingers brushing his on top of the back cushion as I rested my elbow there. The touch sent tingles down my spine, but I slid my hand away, the situation feeling more intimate than either one of us had intended.

"While I took care of the place, though, I'd come up with all these ideas to move the business forward. Modernize it. In hindsight, I realize that changing the business right after my mom passed away was too much for him at the time. Hell, I think leaving was the best thing I ever did, because here? I was angry all the time. Angry that my mom was gone, angry that my pop didn't really let me have a say in anything, even angry at myself that I couldn't seem to let the idea go."

"You were grieving," Cole said softly, a small, sympathetic smile playing at the corners of his mouth.

"Yeah, I guess I was. We both were." I exhaled, cradling my head in the hand that was on the back of the couch. "So, I gave up. I left. And you know what I learned?"

"What?"

I huffed. "My pop was right. I didn't know a damn thing about running a bar or restaurant. You can bet your ass I learned, though, and when I came back here, I had every intention of bringing what I'd learned to Rafferty's. After eight years, he had to have changed his tune…or so I thought. Damn, I had been so naïve."

"Not naïve. Optimistic. Determined to follow your dreams."

If only the rest of the town saw it the way Cole did. "I'd fought for months to get him to change his mind, but after those months and the eight years before, I was done waiting for something that was never going to happen. The warehouse became available and I jumped on it."

"It's amazing, Aiden. I don't know how he can't see how successful you are, that you've built a solid business."

"Thanks." I looked away, not used to sharing so much with someone. Even when I'd been married to Sasha, we didn't talk about the important things. The things that kept me up at night. Talking to Cole, though, was easy.

We spent two more hours in relaxed conversation talking about everything from TV, to politics, to hobbies. Cole showed me pictures of the resin art he made in his spare time. An array of colors and shapes combining wood and resin. They were magnificent and sure as hell more than just a hobby. I even tried to get him to sell me some for the bar, but that was going to take some convincing.

Before I knew it, it was ten o'clock and the streets of Coral Pointe were quiet and dark. I'd had more fun over the last few hours with Cole than I'd had in…I couldn't remember when. Cole helped me clean up the dishes, and there was a pang of disappointment that the night was ending. It may have started as a fake date, but as I walked him to the door, it sure as hell felt real. The palms of my hands were sweaty and I wiped them on my jeans. Nerves fluttered in my stomach, completely ignoring the signals from my brain that they weren't supposed to be there.

Cole opened the door, stepping out onto the landing. Slowly, he faced me, his cheeks slightly pink, adding to the suddenly shy look in his eyes. "I had a really good time tonight. I know it wasn't…you know, like a real date, but…" He shrugged one shoulder, the corner of his mouth lifting in a timid smile. I opened my mouth to disagree, but then he added in a rush, "I'm sure it'll make its way to Drake somehow. Probably when he picks up his morning coffee."

I pressed the heel of my hand to my chest, the reminder of what this night was really about leaving an ache beneath my palm. "Fingers crossed," I managed to say, forcing a smile to my lips. As he turned to walk to his car, I called out his name, stopping him in the middle of the walkway. "I had a really good time, too." The genuine smile I got in return was enough to settle the ache in my chest—at least somewhat.

As I closed the door, my phone rang on the coffee table. Quickly, I grabbed it and slumped down on the couch, answering it. "To what do I owe the honor, Sage?"

"How was your date?"

"It wasn't a date. It was a fake date." As Cole just painfully pointed out.

"*Pfft…* Was there food?"

"Yes."

"Drinks?"

"Yep."

"Get-to-know-you conversation?"

My only answer was a long sigh into the phone.

"That's what I thought. That's a date, cuz. You've just been Saged."

"Still not a thing." I laughed, though, in spite of my sour mood.

"Okay, well then…if it wasn't a date then you'll be perfectly fine with what Cole's signed up for at the festival."

I sat forward, gripping the phone hard. "What do you mean?"

"I just mean…technically, he's single, so it shouldn't matter—"

"Sage, I know where you live," I growled, my voice deeper with an underlying threat I knew he couldn't miss.

"I knew it! I knew you have feelings for him!"

"Sage!" My patience was running thin. After the way the night ended and now with Sage egging me on, I was cranky as hell.

"Okay, okay. So, Cole's mom was in Bluefin tonight with some committee members, and I overheard…" As Sage replayed the conversation he'd eavesdropped on, my hand curled into a fist, my pulse kicking up to dangerous levels.

I didn't know what the hell his mom had been thinking, but her bright idea had disaster written all over it.

CHAPTER 9

COLE

I stared at the patriotically decorated booth surrounded by tents adorned with the same colors, my jaw dropping open. I'd prayed she'd been kidding last night—it had to be a joke, right?—but there was the proof, right in front of my eyes—with a big ol' lip-shaped sign painted red, made out of wood to match the rest of the stand painted blue and white. Who the hell came up with the archaic and, quite frankly, germ-ridden idea of a kissing booth?

"I'm sorry! I just assumed you knew!" Sage said again, rolling his lips in, his cheeks red from the effort of holding in a laugh.

"Does a kissing booth"—I waved at the damn thing, my voice rising an octave until people started staring—"sound like something I'd sign up for, Sage?"

Sage couldn't hold in his laughter anymore, doubling over with his hands pressed to his stomach. "Now that you mention it..."

"What are y'all looking at—*uh oh...*" Levi stood on the other side of Sage, drawing my friend's attention away from my humiliation, Sage's laughter dying down. Anyone who saw the way Sage was looking at Levi right now would have no problem figuring out how Sage felt about the guy. Everyone except Levi, unfortunately.

"Wow, your mom's outdone herself." Ford came up beside me, his wide eyes and dropped jaw more proof that the hideous booth in front of me wasn't a figment of my imagination. He tilted his head to one side then the other, his face scrunched up. "Yeah, dude, you're screwed."

I hung my head, rubbing a hand over my tired eyes as if that would make this all go away. "Fuck. She's lucky this is for a good cause."

Coral Pointe was a lot of things, but sheltered wasn't one of them. The money raised this weekend was going to be divided between three amazing causes—because it would be too easy if Pointers could agree on a single charity. Most of the proceeds would go to an organization for children of fallen soldiers and another to help wounded soldiers. The funds made from Tails of the Sea pet store, the local veterinarian, and randomly—*cringe*—the kissing booth—*double cringe*—would be sent to an organization for rescuing retired military dogs. *Well played, Mom. Using the fact that I'm a sucker for pet adoption against me.* Especially since my allergies kept me from getting a pet of my own.

"Come on," Ford said, gripping my shoulder tightly. "It's not *that* bad."

My head shot up, a narrow-eyed glare aimed at the jackass. "Then you do it."

Before Ford had a chance to answer, Levi jumped in. "Ford has his hands full with the Shore Thing signups. He doesn't have time for…*kissing*."

A cheesy grin split Ford's face as he hiked a thumb at Levi. "What he said."

"Come on, Ford. We still have setting up to do." Levi nudged his head in the direction of Shore Thing Management's tents. Ford slapped my back, shooting me a teasing smile and a wink as he walked away with Levi.

I exhaled, trying to figure out how to fix this debacle my mom had orchestrated—and then I'd find out why the hell she'd put me in this awkward situation, knowing I was seeing Aiden. *Except, you're not really seeing him, jackass. Remember that.* But *she* didn't know that.

"Sage, I need you to do me a favor." When Sage didn't respond, I turned to look at him, struck by the pained confusion in his eyes as he watched Levi and Ford walk away. I placed a hand on his shoulder. "Hey. You okay?"

He finally looked at me. "What? Oh yeah." Sage's eyes found Levi once more, and he released a deep sigh. "I'm fine." His words were about as convincing as unicorns were real. Sage took a deep breath, transforming his face in seconds as he looked back at me, from one of sadness to forced cheerfulness. "What were you saying?"

"Are you sure you're okay?"

Sage blew out a puff of air, swiping a hand in the air. "Yeah, I'm good. What do ya need?"

"Poster board and a Sharpie." If I had to do this damn thing, I was going to do it my way, festival expectations be damned. I was still having trouble figuring out why my mom would do something like this. Of course, the sneaky woman was nowhere to be found, which was oddly convenient since she was on the committee. The fair didn't open for another hour, though. I had work to do at my own tents, and I knew Sage's was already set up and ready to go.

As I weaved through the booths and vendors, I chanced a glance at SandBar's tent, hoping to get a glimpse of the man himself. A twinge of guilt settled in my chest. I hadn't seen Aiden in two days. Okay, I was avoiding him, but with good reason:

Temporary insanity.

Aiden was doing me a massive, life-interfering—his, not mine—generous favor, and here I was, letting my feelings get the best of me. Again.

The other night felt so much like a real date, I was having trouble separating fabrication from truth. There'd been a moment where I could have sworn he was going to kiss me, and holy shit, I'd wanted him to. So, I did the only thing I could think of. I'd brought up Drake—even though he hadn't crossed my mind once that night—to remind myself why Aiden was doing all this for me to begin with. I needed to reassure Aiden that I knew where we stood. It wasn't his fault I had dreams of us wound around each other, all sweaty and sated, until I was a twisted, perpetual pretzel of horniness. His handsome face played through my mind on a loop, how his hair was sliced with gray at the temples. He was going to be one hell of a silver fox.

It wasn't just how sexy he was, though—and he was so fucking sexy. No, it was the way he listened to what I had to say as if it mattered. It was the way he'd brought me my favorite key lime pie, or just the fact that he *knew* it was my favorite to begin with. Or the way he somehow instinctively knew when I was ready to talk about something bothering me and when I wasn't. Or the fact that he didn't push me or criticize me for being so weak when it came to Drake.

Shit.

I couldn't do this again. I couldn't confuse what this was the way I'd confused fucking for intimacy with Drake. Levi was right; I was making what Aiden and I were doing into something it wasn't, and bottom line was, our relationship was nothing more than a lie.

But, that didn't ring true, either. Whatever Aiden and I were, not everything about us was a lie. He was an amazing man and an incredible friend. After the way he'd come to my defense, I was going to do anything to hold on to that friendship, even when the time came to *fake* break up.

A big, meaty hand waved in front of my face, Burke's scowl coming into focus. "Earth to Cole."

Shoving his hand away, I ignored Ford and Noah as they leaned into each other, stifling their laughter.

"Dude's got it bad." Ford shook his head, his hands firmly planted on his hips, his lips quirking up in the corners.

Noah crossed his arms, tilting his head toward Ford. "Seriously. Should we tell him Aiden had to run back to the bar for something?"

"What are you going on about?" I rearranged the condiments on the table for, what had to have been, the twentieth time.

"Don't think we don't see you searching for your lover boy over there." Ford wiggled his eyebrows, nudging his head toward Aiden's tent.

Levi stopped beside me, gripping the back of my neck. "Leave Cole alone. He knows the deal with him and Aiden, right, Cole?"

I was sure the statement was meant to reassure me he had my back. So, why did the comment feel like a sucker punch instead? It wasn't like the thought hadn't just crossed my mind that Aiden and I weren't truly together, but hearing it out loud kind of stung.

"Right." My voice sounded weak, and there was nothing I could do about it. The truth sank like a rock in the pit of my stomach and my hands began to sweat. I was such an enormous jackass because I could see myself falling for Aiden, even though I knew I'd crash and burn once I hit the ground.

"Okay, everyone back to work," Levi ordered, clapping his hands as if to say *chop, chop*.

The next few hours flew by way too quickly. I looked at the time on my phone, dreading the next hour that I had to spend in that fucking kissing booth. I dragged my sorry ass across the way and up the aisle, ignoring the howls of laughter from those assholes formerly known as my friends.

Taking a chance, my gaze slid over to Aiden's tent one more time, my heart skipping a beat when our eyes connected. I waved pathetically, a chill racing down my spine at the intensity in his eyes. If I didn't know any better, that look could kill. That was ridiculous. I hadn't done anything wrong. Hell, I hadn't seen him in days. Maybe he was deciding this was all just too much and I couldn't even blame him. This whole idea was turning into one giant shitshow.

I stopped by Sage's table to pick up the poster I'd asked him to make me. Sage did a double take when he saw me. I knew that twinkle of mischief in his eyes. It was never a good thing when Sage was looking at someone the way he was looking at me right now.

"Did you have a chance to make the sign?" I asked, shifting nervously from foot to foot. I swear I could still feel Aiden's eyes boring a hole in the back of my head. The hair on the back of my neck lifted and my foggy brain wasn't sure whether to be scared or turned on. My dick, however, wasn't confused at all. I shoved my hands in my pockets, discreetly adjusting my semi. Heat rushed to my face as Sage caught the movement and guffawed.

"That excited, huh?" He handed me the rolled up sign, tears lining his eyes from how hard he was laughing.

My head whipped from side to side, a whoosh of air leaving my lungs from relief that no one had apparently been paying attention. "Jesus Christ, Sage."

"What? Are you saying you *aren't* excited for your turn in the Booth of Germs? The Kiss of Death? Lip 'n' Sip?" He cupped his hands around his mouth, leaning his head back as he megaphoned, "*Tongues for Twats?*" I smacked his hands away from his face, while tears streamed down his cheeks again as he laughed at my expense.

"Would you keep it down?" I snorted, unable to keep a straight face. "Did you spend the last few hours coming up with those?"

"'Course I did." Reaching his hand out, Sage handed me a roll of masking tape. Thank god he'd been smart enough to think of it. "Now, shimmy your ass on over to Puckers for Suckers."

I hung my head back and groaned. My mom was in so much trouble—once I found the evil woman.

The second I sat down, relieving my former high school history teacher, I promptly hung my sign on the front of the table. There were a few eye rolls and a couple of snickers, but I didn't give a shit. The only thing I cared about was that the line was blocking my view of Aiden. This was humiliating enough.

AIDEN

Keeping my attention on the customers was a bitch when all I cared about was the fact that Cole was thirty feet away from me, lending those lips to the greedy people of Coral Pointe. The whole thing was absolutely ridiculous. We'd never had a fucking kissing booth at any of our festivals and for good reason. They were inappropriate, unsanitary…and bound to make me lose my damn mind if one more person got in that fucking line.

Worse, the guy was avoiding me, and I had no clue why. I thought our date, real or not, had gone incredibly well the other night, aside from the comment he'd made about Drake finding out. That had hurt more than I cared to admit. Hell, that douche and the reason why Cole had been at my house to begin with had slipped my fucking mind. I'd had more fun with him, told him more than I'd told anyone in Coral Pointe—including Jared. But, the reminder that he wasn't over Drake was a wake-up call that hit me like a ton of bricks. Yet, I couldn't get the guy off my mind. The deep blue of his eyes, the way his skin flushed pink when he was embarrassed or shy, the sound of his laugh.

"Hey, cuz!" Sage called as he approached my table. "Should I see if he wants to borrow my ChapStick?" The little weasel uncapped the small tube and made a show of lathering his lips with the waxy shit then smacked them together with a loud *pop.* He swiped a hand through the air and huffed. "What am I thinking? Guess it doesn't matter which one of us wears it."

"Sage, I'm not above kicking your skinny ass from here to the bouncy castle," I growled, garnering a few laughs from the crowd around us.

"You think my ass is skinny?" He looked over his shoulder down at his ass. Then he stretched his neck to look around the people and down the long aisle to the bouncy castle, his wide eyes turning back to me, his hand on his chest. "My, my, Aiden. Did I hit a nerve?"

He knew damn well he did, just like he had all morning. It was bad enough to know Cole's mom had put her son in that position, but my dear sweet cousin had made sure to pound it in my head all morning. *How many people do you think he'll kiss? Look on the bright side, he's going to make a killing for rescue dogs.* And, of course, *I hope he brought plenty of lip balm.* Needless to say, Billy was my new favorite cousin. And Sage? "Sleep with one eye open tonight."

Sage bent over with obnoxious laughter, wiping tears from his eyes. "Oh, it's just too easy!" He made his way back over to his table, laughing all the way.

Focusing on the task at hand became almost impossible. I forced myself not to watch that line like a fucking hawk. Cole was a grown man. He didn't need me coming to his rescue like some damn possessive Neanderthal. The last thing I wanted to do was drag him away from that stand caveman style. I had a feeling that wouldn't go over very well.

About ten minutes later, I balled my hands tightly when I heard, "Hey, cuz?"

"What now, Sage?" I snapped.

When his serious reply of, "I think you better see something," came out, I spared him a look, my shoulders easing from the sober expression on his face.

Until my eyes followed his, landing on one giant, blond asshole. "No way is he in that fucking line." For someone who was in a fake relationship, I was doing a bang-up job of hiding my raging jealousy and the sudden urge to send that asshole into the inlet by way of my fist.

"This isn't good, Aiden." Sage's whole demeanor changed, his jaw ticking, just as pissed off as I was.

"No, it isn't fucking good, and it's not gonna happen." I untied the apron from around my waist and tossed it on a nearby chair. "Jesse, I'm gonna need you to watch things for a minute." Anger pulsed through every vein in my body as that jackass moved farther up in line. Not waiting for a response, I stormed around the table, hearing Sage say behind me, "Go get 'em, Aiden."

Three rather large steps later, I heard someone calling my name. I sighed, recognizing Irma as she swung her arms and walked briskly in my direction. Apparently, all those power walks paid off. "Hey, Irma."

"Aiden, could you be a doll and get the cooler from my car? My son lifted the heavy thing in for me, but Elise and I just can't seem to carry it, even together."

I looked back toward the line, seeing Drake was seven people away from Cole. *Shitshitshit.*

"Your father wasn't so sure you'd be willing to help, but I assured him you wouldn't let a little old lady fend for herself."

Damn, the woman was good.

"Yeah, sure, Irma. Just, uh, I'm in a hurry so…"

"Right, of course. It's this way."

I followed Irma to her car, keeping an eye on the asshole getting closer and closer to Cole. Popping the trunk open, I grabbed the, admittedly, heavy cooler. How that woman was still driving was anyone's guess. She closed her trunk and I followed her back to her table.

The asshole was now four people away from Cole.

Drake took that moment to turn around and shoot me a shit-eating grin. Taking something out of his pocket, he lifted his hand to his mouth. *What's with all the fucking ChapStick?* A growl from deep in my chest rumbled out as I watched him get his lips ready to kiss *my* boyfriend. *Fake boyfriend, Aiden. Fake.*

Fuck that noise. For all Drake knew, Cole was mine. Over my dead body was he putting his hands—or lips—on what was *mine*.

"You can just set it right there," Irma said. Finally, I tore my gaze away from the asshole. "Thanks so much, dear. I was wondering if you could also—"

"I wish I could, Irma, but I'm really in a hurry." The cooler hit the ground with a bang and I was off again, on a fucking mission. My eyes caught chestnut hair to my right. I flexed my fingers knowing I had to walk a fine line between not having Cole's mom hate me and defending him. When my eyes met hers, I reined in my anger as best as I could, releasing a deep exhale. "Helen, you're gonna have to find a replacement for Cole at that damn booth." Okay, maybe my delivery could have been a little better, but I got my point across loud and clear. Cole's mom looked to the booth, worrying her bottom lip when she saw who was in line. *Yeah, brilliant idea.*

I didn't wait for her response, my heart thundering in my chest to see that there was only one person between Drake and Cole's forbidden lips. Bypassing the line and dirty looks from patrons, I sidled up next to Teresa, digging in my pocket for the crumpled up bills. This was about to be her lucky day. "Teresa, you wouldn't mind if I cut in line, would you?"

I caught the shock in Cole's eyes as he stood there slack-jawed, noticed the way his face had gone pale. His eyes drifted from me to Drake and back to me. This was either going to be astronomically amazing or go down in a ball of flames.

"The line starts back there, Rafferty." Drake's voice grated on me, the hairs on my arms and neck standing on end.

I shot him the finger over my shoulder, not sparing him the smallest of glances. "Tell that to your boyfriend, *Myers*, and leave mine the hell alone." Cole sucked in a sharp breath, his tongue darting out to moisten those pink lips.

Luckily, Teresa took that moment to say, "I don't mind, Aiden. Not. At. All." She fanned her rosy cheeks, looking back and forth between me and Cole.

Dropping money on the table—hell, I wasn't even sure how much—I leaned over the one foot of wood separating us, took Cole's shocked face in my hands, and pulled his lips to mine. I heard the gasps and whispers around us, and Drake's snarled, "You've got to be fucking kidding me," behind me. The sounds faded away when Cole's stiff lips finally loosened and moved with mine, a sweet little whimper escaping him.

Holy. Fucking. Hell. Was someone setting off fireworks? There had to be fireworks somewhere, as bright lights exploded behind my eyes. I didn't deepen the kiss, despite every nerve ending in my body screaming at me to do just that. I wanted to taste him. I wanted to explore whatever the hell this was—but I didn't want an audience, and I knew Cole wouldn't either. No, if there were going to be any more whimpers, they were going to be for my ears only.

"Oh sweet baby Jesus," Teresa whispered, reminding me she was standing next to me.

Cole puffed out a laugh against my mouth, so satisfying and

pure, I fucking soared. He leaned his forehead against mine, my thumb still brushing over the slight stubble of his cheek. The feel of it against my skin was new, but definitely something I could get used to. "So, um…that was…"—he licked his lips again—"nice. *Really* nice."

"Yeah. Yeah, it was." Reluctantly, I released him and took a step back. "Let's get out of here. I already told your mom she needs to find someone else." Reaching for his hand on the outside of the booth, it was then I noticed the sign in front of me. I barked out a laugh as I read it.

Two dollars to help save a pet,
But a kiss on the cheek is all you get.

"I have my limits," Cole said, laughter in his voice, his hand in mine, right where it was meant to be.

"I'm learning mine aren't what they used to be," I said softly, studying his eyes for any signs that he wasn't okay with what I'd just done.

Cole finally replied, "You'll hear no complaints from me," and I released the breath I'd been holding.

I'd fallen victim to the kissing booth trap, and I couldn't find an ounce of regret.

CHAPTER 10

COLE

I walked back to my tent in a daze, my lips still tingling from Aiden's kiss. *Did that really just happen?* I lifted my fingers, brushing them over my mouth as it curved into a cheesy smile.

When I'd noticed Drake in line at the booth, my heart plummeted and my hands began to shake. Pouty Water Kid nowhere in sight, the only thing that had accompanied Drake was the determined look in his eyes. Determined to humiliate me some more? Determined to prove a point? Make me see what I'd been missing? Prove I was a bad kisser? I didn't know what the hell he'd been up to, or why, but whatever it was would only end badly for me. I had no doubt about that.

But…Aiden pushing his way through the crowd, looking like he was about to murder someone? Holy unexpected. It had taken seconds for my attention to be yanked from Drake and latch onto Aiden like a barnacle. The determination in his eyes had been confusing, but I'd welcomed it with a thrill of anticipation.

And the moment our lips had met…

I've heard people spout nonsense about seeing stars or feeling like they were floating on air. I'd thought it was a bunch of bullshit, until Aiden's lips touched mine and I swore my feet had left the ground. I'd felt astoundingly weightless, my mind trying to catch up as all blood rushed to the nerve endings on my lips and farther south. I wasn't big on public displays of affection, but in that moment, I'd been ready to add exhibitionism to my list of accomplishments. It gave new meaning to Puckers for Suckers, that was for sure.

"Holy shit, Cole!" Sage hopped up and down next me, falling into stride by my side. "That was epic!"

I side-glanced at Sage, my cheeks burning as I tried to calm the pure giddiness I was feeling. "It was something, alright."

"That's it? That's all you have to say? Aiden just—"

I stopped short, making Sage bounce right off me. "Aiden just kissed his boyfriend?" I gave him the eye, hoping he'd get the hint. My gaze darted around nervously, afraid our cover had been blown. I hated that I still needed to hide behind the safety of Aiden, but the way I just froze when faced with Drake proved I wasn't ready to do this on my own yet.

Sage's head went back, a long *ooooh* releasing as he caught on. "Right, and it absolutely wasn't the first time you kissed. Nope. You kiss all the time. Just kiss, kiss, kiss." Sage winked, but in trying to make it better, he was only making it worse.

"You need to work on your subtlety." I patted him on the head.

He immediately pushed my hand away. "Whatever." And then in a softer voice he said, "Sooo…?"

"Are you really asking me what it's like to kiss your cousin?" I laughed, throwing my arm up defensively to block Sage's smack.

Sage rolled his eyes dramatically with a sigh to match. "Don't be gross, asswipe. You know what I'm asking."

I started walking toward Shore Thing Management's tables

again, knowing he would follow. "Yes, I know what you're asking, and yes, it was *that* amazing. Can we stop talking about this now?"

"Was that so difficult? I swear, you and Aiden need to work on your chill…behind closed doors…with a bed…" I stopped short, my eyes darting around, my cheeks the temperature of lava. Sage put his hands up and backed away. "I'm just sayin'."

It was my turn to roll my eyes, shaking my head as I continued on to my tables while Sage went back to his. Of course, I had more of the same waiting for me.

"Oh *ho*! Look who it is!" Ford slapped my back, forcing me to take a step forward. "We heard your boyfriend broke you out of jail."

"*Pfft*...that's not all we heard," Noah said, closing in on my other side. "We really do miss everything, Ford."

Ford gestured in front of me to Noah on my other side. "I'm sayin'! What the hell?"

"If it's any consolation, I had no idea it was coming"—I gave my best friends a wicked smile—"but I sure as hell caught up."

"Yeah ya did," Ford nodded, pride radiating from him.

My phone buzzed in my pocket, my cheeks hurting from how much I was smiling when I read the text from Aiden while trying to hide my screen. **Get a drink with me after we close up?**

The idea was tempting, but…**You know we'll have an audience at the bar.**

Aiden's answer was immediate. **My place then. 10?**

I'll be there.

"What are you smiling about? Unless you're gonna share with the class, get your ass in gear and serve some food," Burke barked at me then focused on Ford and Noah. "Y'all have no excuse. Get back to your table."

Ford stood ramrod straight, giving Burke a, "Sir! Yes, Sir!" and a salute, yelping as Burke smacked his ass when he passed by. "Sir, yes, *Sir*..." he purred, wiggling his eyebrows and holding a hand over the cheek Burke had just smacked. A boisterous laugh came from the grumpy man, the crowd of people witnessing their antics joining in.

No doubt, there were some who questioned whether any of us were fucking. Truth was, we'd never ever crossed that line. We were like brothers, but the teasing was over-the-top and sometimes came off as flirty. To us, we just had fun; we were ourselves with each other.

I thought about being with Aiden the other night. It had been awkward at first, especially with my nervous blabbermouth, but by the end of the night, I felt as comfortable with him as I was with these guys. Difference was, I didn't want to see what it took to make their eyes roll back in their heads or their toes curl. *How do you know you have what it takes to make Aiden's do that?* According to Drake, I *didn't* have what it took. Swallowing hard, I considered canceling my plans with Aiden that night but pushed the thought aside when a group came over to our table.

As we were closing up, that thought viciously resurfaced, and I came close to punching a message in my phone telling Aiden I couldn't make it tonight. Luckily, my friends knew when to tease me and when I needed an ear.

"What's up, man? You okay?" Burke asked, giving me the softer side of him not many people got to see. Burke pulled a chair over, signaling for the others to come closer. It was after nine, but we'd closed down most of the table. The tents were staying up for the following two days.

Making sure we were relatively alone, I sank down into a chair across from Burke and waited for them all to sit before I poured my heart out—or, at least tried to. "I..." Gripping the back of my neck, I searched for the words, deciding I wasn't outing Aiden if I truly didn't know where he stood to begin with. Besides, he'd basically outed himself...twice now. "I don't know if I'm reading this wrong, but…I think maybe Aiden's"—I looked around one more time, making sure we were alone—"not as straight as he thought he was."

"Cole, the dude kissed you in front of everyone. I think it's safe to say he's probably not." Ford, usually the jokester of our group, looked at me with complete sincerity. "What makes you think you're reading him wrong?"

Before I could think better of it, my eyes darted to Levi, guilt slamming me when Ford, Noah, and Burke simultaneously shot him what-the-fuck scowls and Levi flinched. "Don't look at me like that," Levi retorted, returning the scowl. "I just want him to be careful. Drake really fucked with his head. Is it so bad that I don't want him to get into another situation where he feels more than the other person?" Levi's eyes drifted to Ford, but I wasn't sure anyone noticed but me, and I didn't know what to make of it. "I don't want him to get hurt."

Burke, Ford, and Noah dropped the scowls, nodding their agreement.

"Uh, *he's* right here." Jesus, what was with people talking about me like I wasn't there? "I'm not saying I'm in love with the guy, but I'm getting some seriously mixed signals and I don't know what to do."

Noah leaned forward, gripping my shoulder. "First of all, breathe." I took a deep breath, letting it out slowly through my nose. "Second of all," he continued, "I highly doubt he would've done what he did today if he wasn't questioning what he's feeling. We weren't able to see the kiss, but we sure as hell saw the fire coming out of his ears before he went storming off in your direction. He was jealous, Cole. Plain as fucking day."

"But why would he be?" I couldn't wrap my brain around it. Aiden had never before given hints that he was attracted to men. Why me?

"Why wouldn't he be?" Levi's brows pinched a line between

them. "Look, I know I said to be careful, but Noah's right. He was a man on a mission today."

I remembered what he'd looked like when he came over to the booth, how he'd called me his boyfriend in front of Drake. Hell, in front of everyone. He hadn't even noticed the sign I'd hung up, just went straight in for the kiss. My skin prickled, heat pooling in my groin.

"Don't overthink it." Burked leaned forward, resting one forearm on his thigh and placing his other hand on my knee. "See how he is with you tomorrow."

"Tonight," I said, enjoying their confusion until I added. "He asked me to stop by tonight for a drink."

"Way to bury the lead, Cole." Ford laughed and shook his head. "Yeah, I'd say the guy is interested, 'cause I love you guys, but I'm fucking tired after today. Ain't no way in hell I'd want company tonight."

The other three voiced their agreement. Maybe they were right, but I wasn't going to find out unless I stopped overthinking it and got the hell out of here.

I checked the time on my phone and jumped up from my chair. "I gotta go. I want to stop home for a quick shower." Ignoring their teasing innuendo, I left them there to finish up, racing to my car.

By the time I knocked on Aiden's door, the butterflies were back with a vengeance. *I can be in my car and in the safety of my home in less than...*

"Hi," Aiden greeted me when he swung the door open, and it hit me suddenly that the broad smile on his face was for me. That smile faltered when I failed to respond.

I rushed out a, "Hi," back, relieved to see the tension in his expression ease.

"Come on in." Aiden moved aside so I could walk past him. He smelled fresh and clean, his dark hair still damp from the shower. He looked refreshed, even though I knew he had to be as exhausted as I was. He'd changed into a plain, navy blue T-shirt and jeans, looking sexier than I'd ever seen him. It never impressed me when a guy cared too much about designer this and that. Not that there was anything wrong with it; Noah and Levi wore it well—and Drake, well he just wore it. It just wasn't my thing.

"How about a glass of wine? It's a little late for a beer."

He had to have caught me checking him out. It wasn't like I was being all super stealthy about it—there wasn't *anything* super stealthy about me—but he didn't seem like it weirded him out.

"Sounds good to me." I followed him into his kitchen, my heart stuttering when I saw the wooden board with an array of cheeses, meats, and grapes. The arrangement was so simple, yet the effort he'd put into it screamed *date*.

I took the glass of wine he offered me. Aiden held his and picked up the board with his free hand, leading me into the living room. My damn pulse was thumping a hard rhythm, and my nerves were having a fucking dance party. We both sat down on the couch, one of my knees bouncing.

"Was your mom upset with me?"

My knee jerked to a stop. "Why would she be mad at you?"

"Well, I wasn't exactly friendly when I told her she needed to find a replacement for you, but Drake was in that damn line and…" He shrugged, a sheepish smile on his face. "You know the rest."

I sure did. I swear, my lips were still tingling. "I didn't see her, but I have every intention of finding her tomorrow and asking her what she was thinking. She crossed a line this time." I scrunched up my face. "And, she knows I'm dating you—I mean…you know what I mean."

"Wouldn't be the first time someone didn't like me, I guess."

Aiden rubbed the back of his neck and sighed. "Not a great feeling, though, considering…"

My hand landed on his knee. "I'll talk to her, Aiden. She needs to respect my decisions, and I'll be damned if she's going to disrespect you. For all she knows, you and I are really together." A part of me wished it was true.

A few sips of wine—in silence—later, I was officially on edge and wondering what the hell I was doing here. *Just ask him.* I took a deep breath, let it out, and said, "What are we doing, Aiden?"

Wow, I shocked the hell out of even myself. With Drake, I'd never had the nerve to ask him what we were, too afraid to rock the boat. But with Aiden, the need to know what was going on between us was stronger than my fear of what the answer might be. It hit me that I was already more comfortable with Aiden than I had ever been with Drake, because with Aiden, I was starting to feel stronger, not weaker.

"Honestly? I'm not sure. I guess I'm trying to figure it all out."

"Figure what out? If you're attracted to me? Guys in general?" Was being someone's experiment any better than being someone's back-up plan? "Because, I gotta tell you, this isn't feeling so fake."

Aiden's gorgeous smile left me breathless. "Oh, I'm attracted to you. No doubt about that."

That…was not what I was expecting him to say. "You are?"

He took a slow sip of his wine, his Adam's apple bobbing as he swallowed, his eyes never leaving mine. I'd never wanted to be a liquid more in my life, just to know what it was like to slide down that throat. Aiden studied me, and I swear I felt his eyes travel over me like a caress. "Yeah, Cole. I definitely am."

Jesus Christ this man… My mouth was completely dry, hands

shaking as I took a sip of wine to coat my parched tongue. "How are you so okay with this?"

Aiden shrugged a shoulder casually. "I've never really been one to overthink things too much."

"So, you're impulsive?" Did my voice really have to sound so small and unsure?

He set his wine glass down, slid closer to me, then took my glass and set it next to his. Aiden held my hands in his, my pulse kicking up even harder, faster, my brain malfunctioning with how close he was to me. "No, I'm not impulsive. I just listen to what my heart and my mind are telling me. Losing my mom taught me that tomorrow isn't promised. It would be a real fucking tragedy if I'd held myself back from something I wanted just because it's new. Can it be scary? Absolutely. Doesn't mean it isn't worth going after anyway. I'm thirty-eight years old and still learning new things about myself every single day."

"You make it sound so simple."

"Not simple, just…lessons learned, I guess." He said it as if it wasn't impressive but, man, was I impressed. Aiden squeezed my hands, all confidence draining from his demeanor, replaced with something akin to trepidation. "I need to ask you something, though."

"Okay…"

"Today…that kiss… Were you okay with it? Because I would never make you do—"

I don't know what came over me, but I didn't wait for the rest. My mouth crashed into his, stealing a kiss seconds before I reared back in horror. Sucking in a breath, I floundered for an apology, pushing myself back on the couch to put space between us. Darkness overtook his green eyes, his fist gripping the front of my shirt as he yanked me closer, slamming his mouth over mine.

All other thoughts ceased to exist except the feel of his warm lips. There was no way my body was letting my brain drive this time. I let out an embarrassing whimper when his tongue brushed my bottom lip, an even bigger moan when that delicious tongue slid into my mouth, gliding around mine. He was kissing me. He was *actually* kissing me. There wasn't an audience, the dick who shall remain nameless was nowhere in sight, and Aiden was truly kissing me.

The man permeated all of my senses…the silken taste of cabernet on his tongue, the freshly showered fragrance of his warm skin, his soft hair as I pushed my fingers through it and held on, and the small grunt he made as he took the kiss even deeper. He was everywhere and yet I searched for more of him. Aiden gave himself willingly, moving over me until my back was pressed to the couch. He never let up the welcome invasion of lips and tongue. His body, however, hovered above me, stiff body language warning me he was unsure about crossing that line. If he'd never been with a man before, this was completely uncharted territory for him.

Reluctantly, I pulled my mouth away, asking through gasps of air, "Are you sure you want this?"

His brow furrowed, a flash of…hurt, maybe?…crossed his face. "Yeah, I am. Do you?"

Aiden was right. Listening to what my mind and my heart were telling me, I yanked him back down, but this time I pulled his full weight on top of me. A grunt tore out of him when I spread my legs, letting him fall between them.

"Fuck." His breath shuddered against my mouth as I lifted my hips, pressing my erection against his. He was fucking hard. If I had any doubt before about his attraction, that swollen dick rocking against mine shattered it into a million pieces. "Here I am, pointing out I'm thirty-eight, and all I want to do is rub off on you until we both explode in our jeans like horny teens."

"Jesus, Aiden," I replied, a little in awe and a whole hell of a lot turned on. I licked my lips and stared into the wonder shining from his eyes. "It's your move. I'll like whatever you do, but just so you know…I'm not opposed to pushing the barriers out of the way." My words filtered through his brain before his eyes darkened with understanding. A couple of heartbeats passed, and my bravado deflated. Had I pushed him too far?

CHAPTER 11

AIDEN

I sucked in a breath, then another, trying to convince my dick not to blow before we even got to the good stuff. Cole offering himself up like that had to be the sexiest thing I'd ever seen. He was still cautious, I could see it in his eyes. He'd been hurt before, yet he was willing to put himself out there. For me. I had a feeling he wasn't used to being vocal about what he wanted out of sex. The courage it took for him to voice it now—was there anything hotter than that?

Cole's eyes shifted away, and I cursed myself for waiting so long that he was doubting himself. I'd be damned if I was the cause, especially because we were *definitely* on the same page. Leaning down again, I claimed his mouth, working another sweet whimper out of him. Letting my body take the lead, I followed willingly as my hips moved, eliciting another moan from us both. Cole fisted the back of my shirt, pulling me closer at the same time. I knew what he was saying without words… It wasn't enough. We both needed more, and there was only one way to achieve that.

Wedging my hand between us, I raised my hips enough to get to the button of his jeans. His blue eyes grew wide then settled into a half-lidded stare that shot straight to my cock. That willingness to give himself over to me made every cell in my body sing. I worked the button through the hole one-handed, pulled the zipper down slowly, and spread the material apart. Royal blue cotton over a swollen mound between his legs made my mouth run dry. It was safe to say I wanted it. I so fucking wanted it.

Gently, I brushed my fingers over his erection, fascinated by the wet spot on his underwear near his tip. I rubbed my fingers over it, grazing the head of his cock in the process. His breathing kicked up, hips pushing his cock into my hand as he bit his bottom lip. "You like that?" I asked, running my thumb over the spot again, reveling in the small squeak and frantic nod of his head. I did it a few more times, my pulse pounding when he finally lifted trembling fingers to my jeans, opening them the way I did his.

I took his mouth again, swiping my tongue inside the wet heat, pressed our erections together. It was amazing, but with the thin layers of cotton still separating us, it wasn't enough. Taking a chance, I growled, pulling my shirt up under my chin and pushing my jeans and underwear down enough to release my dick. I met his eyes, watched the blue deepen as they dilated and focused on my cock. My legs and arms trembled when he reached out a finger, swiped the bead of pearly white liquid from my slit, and brought it to his mouth. His eyes slid closed as he tasted me, like it was a delicacy melting on his tongue.

"Fuck, that's sexy," I whispered, claiming his lips again, my tongue sweeping inside to taste myself in the hot cavern of his mouth. His hands shifted between us, pushing his own shirt up before moving lower to work his pants down around his thighs. Sensations fired off in my system when he pulled my hips down until we were skin on hot skin, cock to glorious cock. "Holy shit,"

I groaned, screwing my eyes shut so as not to shoot off before I even got my hips moving.

"Yeah," he whispered, taking the initiative, sliding his cock alongside mine. My whole fucking world changed in that one, take-charge decision. This time he kissed me, sparking me into action.

I let my full weight press him into the couch, my brain finally catching up, my hips surging forward. Cole broke the kiss for a moment, licked the palm of his hand, then pushed his tongue back in my mouth while shoving his hand between us. I felt wet heat surround me, his warm hand dragging through our pre-come and around us both, making the glide of our cocks easier.

Taking the lead, I jerked my hips forward and back. Our breaths came in fast pants, too fast to keep up the rhythm of kissing. I buried my face in his neck, and his fist gripped the back of my shirt, fingers digging into my skin through the material. Heat raced down my spine, the intensity growing quickly and my frantic need to come shooting to my toes and back up again. I was losing control, but the need to get Cole to come first was like a living, breathing thing inside me. A demand to know he was feeling what I was feeling. That the orgasm balancing on the edge of my sanity would be matched by the release I was hoping to pull from him.

Cole froze beneath me, and I lifted up in time to see his head pushed back on the couch pillow, eyes screwed shut, mouth open on a sexy groan. Wet heat pumped between us as he coated my cock, my orgasm ripping through me, my release joining his on our skin. "Oh fuck…*fuck…*" I shuddered, dragging in deep breaths as I tried to come back down to earth, my body still shaking.

There was a mess pressed between us, but I didn't care. I kissed him slowly this time, shifting my body toward the back of the couch, only enough so I wasn't resting all of my weight on him. Cole was in shape and lean, but I outweighed him by at least fifteen pounds. Our cocks rested against his thigh, completely sated. I stared at them, in absolute awe of what we'd just done.

"Was that okay?" Cole's soft voice filtered through my foggy, sex-satisfied brain.

I met his eyes, ready to make a joke about how completely *okay* it was to be covered in come—until I met the unease there. "Was that…? Are you serious?" I figured the orgasm I'd shouted out minutes before and the come drying on our stomachs was enough proof, but there was nothing but doubt in his eyes.

Cole shrugged one shoulder and averted his gaze. "It's been brought to my attention recently that I may not be as great at sex as I thought I was."

My blood fucking boiled. "I really hate that asshole." Placing a finger on his jaw, I turned his head toward me. "You're hot as fuck, Cole, especially when you take the lead. There wasn't a single second of what just happened that wasn't *okay*. It was better than okay. It was amazing." Thing was, I was the newbie here when it came to sex with another guy. Sure, we'd both got off, but maybe it wasn't as great as I thought it was? "Did you think it was okay?" I asked, feeling stupid for the sudden surge of doubt. I wasn't usually one to doubt my abilities when it came to sex. I knew every which way to get a woman to scream my name, but this was a whole different ball game. You'd think it would be easier to gauge, having the same body parts, but everything with Cole felt new.

Cole's face scrunched, shock replacing worry on his face. "It was amazing for me, too."

"Okay then." I smiled, leaning down to steal another kiss.

"I guess we just slid into friends-with-benefits territory, huh?"

Ouch. I mean, I really couldn't blame him. Technically, we were still fake dating, and I was the one who told him I wasn't exactly sure what we were doing, that I was still trying to figure everything out. I didn't want to scare him by admitting that what just happened between us made things a whole lot clearer. "Not the worst place to be in, especially with you."

That garnered me a small smile that was really hard to read. Was he okay with it? Disappointed? "Agreed." A yawn escaped that mouth I'd just kissed the hell out of. "Sorry. It's been a really long day."

"What time do you have to be up tomorrow?"

He thought for a second. "I have to stop at the inn and make sure things are okay before going to the festival, so early. I should probably get going." He winced with the last sentence, most likely worried that I'd think he was bailing after sex. Not gonna lie, the thought crossed my mind, but I shoved it away.

"Don't move," I said, maneuvering myself over him until one foot hit the floor. I pushed myself up, yanking my shirt over my head before it slid down into the mess on my stomach. I tucked my cock back in, not bothering to close my jeans. Everything was coming off soon anyway. Tossing my shirt onto my bedroom floor as I passed by it, I opened the linen closet outside the bathroom and grabbed a washcloth, wetting it with warm water.

As I entered the living room again, Cole was just about to pull his pants back up, but I rushed over, my hand hovering over his crotch until I thought better of it. Awkwardly, I handed him the towel, letting him clean himself up. A pang of regret filtered through as I watched him, wishing I'd done that for him. Man, there was so much I needed to figure out with Cole. So much I *wanted* to figure out.

He shyly handed the towel back to me then tucked himself away, righting his clothes. When he got to my front door, me following behind, he stopped. "I, uh…" he said, his eyes flicking down to my bare chest, licking his lips. Holy hell, what that did to me. Cole shook his head, as if trying to snap out of it. "I'll see you tomorrow?" It was a question instead of a definitive statement. He was still unsure about all of this. I guess, in a way, so was I.

I was sure about one thing, though. "I'll see you tomorrow." I wasn't sure if it was a friends-with-benefits thing to do, but I didn't care. I leaned in, kissing him softly one more time. Apparently, it was the right thing to do, going by the smile he gave me when I pulled back.

As I lay in bed that night and stared at the ceiling, one hand tucked underneath my head, I realized I had figured something out. A few things, actually.

First, I liked dick—at least Cole's dick. Not in a…*that wasn't bad*…kind of way. In a…*I can't wait to figure out all the ways I can make Cole come*…kind of way.

Second, Drake had done a fucking number on Cole's head. The guy went from making me come harder than I had in a long time, to worrying it hadn't been good enough. That wasn't going to fly. I'd make sure of it.

And, the last thing I realized, as I turned onto my side, sliding my hand under my pillow, was that friends-with-benefits was a shit title. I intended to upgrade, as soon as I could convince Cole to give us a chance…because there was no going back. At least not for me.

I worked at the fair the next morning, my eyes drifting over to Cole repeatedly over the hours. We hadn't really had a chance to talk, Saturday being the busiest day of the festival, but I was rewarded with a few shy smiles. I soaked every one of them in. For a fraction of a second, I worried I was being too obvious. Then I remembered people thought we were together. Damned if I didn't look my fill after that.

I had to rein myself in occasionally, though. Looking my fill meant remembering that lean body beneath mine, the way our slick cocks had slotted together perfectly, the sound he'd made when he'd come.

I adjusted myself for the umpteenth time that morning, rolling my eyes when I caught the devilish grin Sage was giving me as he approached my table.

"Well, well, well...someone looks happy." He stopped with his hands on his hips, studying me way too carefully with narrowed eyes. "*Very* happy."

"Alert the media! Aiden Rafferty is happy." I gave him a wry smile.

Sage moved closer to the table, his voice dropping lower. "You know what you're doing, cuz?"

A snarky comment about asking Cole if I knew what I was doing last night was on the tip of my tongue. Somehow, innuendo seemed to lessen what had happened between us. I blew out a breath, glancing down the aisle at Cole again, his bright smile making something in my stomach flutter. "I'm trying to figure it out," I said truthfully. When Sage opened his mouth, I added, "And, yes, Cole knows. Believe me, hurting him is the last thing I want to do."

Sage must have been satisfied with either my answer or the look on my face...or both...because his face lit up with pride. "Good. You should have seen the daggers Drake was shooting you when you kissed Cole yesterday. I'm telling you, that man was fuming. I have a feeling he's not gonna let this go so easily."

I snorted. "I don't get it. He treated Cole like shit, made it clear he didn't want him, and now he's pissed because he doesn't have him? What the fuck kind of logic is that?" I tossed an empty beer bottle in the can next to me a little too forcefully, the sound of glass shattering punctuating the anger racing over me. Seriously, what the hell was that guy's problem?

"It's not logic. It's jealousy and pride. He's a spoiled brat and you took away his toy. All I'm sayin' is, watch your back."

A puff of air left my mouth as I shook my head in disbelief. "I'm not worried. Trust me, I can handle Drakeula." A laugh burst out of Sage and I grinned. "What? Isn't that what you guys call him?"

"Uncle Jim! Are you okay?"

My head jerked to my left, the frantic sound of my cousin Billy's voice piercing through the noise of the crowd. I dropped the bottle in my hand and ran over to the Rafferty's table, my heart lurching in my chest to see my pop sitting in a chair, pressing a hand to his chest.

"Pop, are you okay?" I asked, dropping to my knees on the ground in front of him.

He brushed me off, scowling at Billy to his right. "I said I was fine. Billy's just being dramatic."

If looks could kill… "Watch it, old man," she snapped. "You keep saying you're fine, yet this seems to keep happening."

That caught my attention, my legs shaky as I stood up, ignoring the crowd forming around us. "Keeps happening? What are you talking about?"

"I said it's nothing. Just some heartburn." He waved a hand in the air. "Go on back over to your table. Nothing to see here." The word *table* dripped with disgust.

Dismissed—fucking *again*—in front of an entire crowd of nosey Pointers. My hands flexed, the urge to tell the old man off right then and there bouncing its way to my mouth. Before I could say something I would, undoubtedly, regret, a warm hand slid into mine, another gripping my bicep.

Cole.

I took a deep breath, squeezing his hand, soaking in the comfort he was giving me. Pop's eyes dropped to our linked hands and he shook his head and looked away. The disapproval hurt just as much as, if not more than, the dismissal a few seconds before. Cole must have seen it, too, his hold on my hand loosening. I was having none of that, gripping his hand even tighter.

Fuck if I was going to let my pop make me feel guilty for the one bright spot in my life right now.

Anything I said to him would have a huge audience of people ready to misconstrue my words. Anger drained from my body, my shoulders slumping in defeat. I turned, ready to walk away, when Cole held on, keeping me in place. "He loves you, ya know, despite how you treat him. He loves you." I sucked in a breath, as did other people in the crowd, staring at Cole in fucking awe. No one had ever defended me like that with my pop before, and sure as hell not in public.

Cole didn't wait for a response, tugging on my hand to pull me from the throng of people getting their daily dose of gossip at my expense. By the time we made it back to my table, I found my voice again. "I can't believe you just did that."

Uncertainty creased Cole's forehead, an apology forming on his lips. I took his face in my hands, brushing my thumbs over the short stubble on his cheeks. "Thank you." Going on instinct, I kissed him softly, lingering for a few seconds before reluctantly pulling away.

"A-anytime," he stuttered, a glowing smile forming as the shock began to melt away.

"Aiden, I'm really sorry to break this up," Jesse said, "but you were supposed to be at the bar ten minutes ago. Jeff has to leave."

"Shit," I muttered, leaning my forehead on Cole's. "I gotta go. I'll talk to you later?"

Cole nodded, that gorgeous smile still on his face. "Later."

CHAPTER 12

COLE

"Mom, if you don't call me back, you're never getting grandbabies, and you and I both know I'm your only shot." I ended the call to snickers from the guys.

"Damn, Cole…pullin' out the big guns." Ford hooked an arm around my neck. "You're on a roll today. I'm a little turned on."

I shoved his arm off me, laughing. "Shut up. This is ridiculous! The woman is avoiding me!" I'd kept my eyes out for her all morning with the exception of the scene with Aiden's dad. I still couldn't believe I'd said anything at all, but one look at Aiden's dejected face and the urge to protect him broke through the surface of any fear I might've had. He didn't deserve to be treated the way his dad had treated him, especially in front of all of Coral Pointe. I'd never known anyone to be as stubborn as Jim.

My mom, however, took home the prize of Most Meddlesome. She'd avoided me for a solid day, which really only proved she knew what she'd done was wrong.

I found my dad's contact in my phone and hit send. He answered on the second ring. "Hey, Cole. How's the festival going?" He owned the small pharmacy in town, and had been the pharmacist there for the last thirty years. He'd always *had* to work on the handfuls of festivals Coral Pointe had throughout the year. Did I mention he was smart?

"Well, let's see…"

"Oh boy… What did my beautiful wife do this time?"

"Two words, Dad. Kissing Booth. That's right, she signed me up for a freaking kissing booth!"

His laugh came through the speaker of my phone so loud and clear, Burke and Levi standing next to me joined in.

"It's not funny!" But I couldn't hold the laugh in. The woman was relentless, but I loved her anyway. "She knows I'm seeing Aiden. Why would she do that?" I sucked in a breath, my words sounding more like fact than fiction.

"Aiden…?" He was quiet for a second. "Aiden Rafferty?"

"Um…yeah?" I squeaked. Now I was officially lying to both my parents. And I thought my mom was bad?

"That's great, Cole. I wasn't aware he's gay—"

"Bi."

He chuckled. "Either way, I'm happy for you. He's a great man. Does this mean I get the family discount on Whale of an Ale? That's a damn good beer."

I hung my head and laughed. "Let's not get ahead of ourselves, okay? It's still…*really* new, but Mom needs to back off. I'd tell her so myself, but the woman is avoiding me."

"Last night makes so much more sense now. Usually she comes home from those things and fills me in on all the gossip I wasn't sad to miss to begin with. But, instead, she went straight to bed."

"Mmmhmm…the mark of a guilty woman."

He barked a laugh into the phone again. "You sit tight. Your mom will be in front of your tent in five minutes. I guarantee it."

I didn't know what he was up to, but I knew whatever it was, it would work. "Thanks."

Sure enough, five minutes later, my mom was pushing through the crowd, old people with canes and baby carriages be damned. "Cole! Cole, are you okay? Your father said you fainted and hit your head."

I snorted while she searched me over, looking for something she was never going to find. When she pulled away confused, I crossed my arms over my chest and quirked a brow with a smirk. "So your phone works after all. Good to know."

She pulled back with a sheepish frown and smacked my arm. "Don't you scare me like that again."

"I didn't. Dad did. Now that I have your attention, though…" I linked my arm through hers to prevent her escape. "Y'all, my mom and I are gonna go for a little walk. I'll be back in a few."

You'd think she'd be anxious, but she wasn't too nervous to tilt her head and point to her cheek as she passed by Burke and Levi. The traitors each obliged and kissed her on the cheek, warming my heart regardless of the fact that she was in trouble. I loved that she'd taken to Burke, Ford, Levi, and Noah as if they were her own. My parents had trouble conceiving me, therefore, siblings hadn't been an option. Now she had five men to mother. To say she was elated was an understatement.

That thought managed to fuel my anger even more with the way she was handling me seeing Aiden. Once we were mostly out of earshot, I faced her. "What do you have against Aiden?"

She stared at me incredulously. "What are you talking about? I don't have anything against Aiden."

"That stunt you pulled yesterday says otherwise. You don't think that was out of line considering I told you I was in a relationship with him? And, did it even occur to you that it was putting me right in Drake's line of fire?"

She looked down. "Well, no. I hadn't considered that part."

That part? "But the Aiden part crossed your mind and you did it anyway? Or was it *because* of Aiden you did it?"

She wouldn't meet my eyes, didn't respond, and my heart sank. If she had a problem with him, like so many people here, because of Jim Rafferty, this was going to stop right now.

"Mom, Aiden is a good man. One of the best I know. I can't believe you'd do something like that. What were you thinking?"

Her eyes snapped up to me, giving me the look she'd given me so many times over the years when I was in trouble. I wasn't caving this time. "What I was thinking was I don't want another man using my son."

I reared back. "What?"

"Aiden Rafferty has been straight all his life. Why now? Why you?" she asked in a huff. I winced, hating that she'd asked the question I'd asked myself only yesterday. "I'll tell you *why you*. Because you are the sweetest, most caring man I know besides your father. You give and you give, and what do you get in return?"

"Mom…"

"No, Cole. I will not sit by while another man hurts my baby. Drake, that lowlife piece of you know what, broke your heart over and over again and I stood by helpless. I'll be damned if Aiden does the same thing. The man isn't gay, so tell me, what does he get out of all this? I hear his bar has been busier than ever."

I took a step back with a gasp, rubbing the heel of my hand over my chest. A niggling pebble of doubt began to form. I shoved it back down as best I could.

"First he turns his back on his family, and when that's not good enough, he uses you to create a buzz big enough to give him a boost in sales." She laughed humorously. "Well, it won't happen. Not if I have anything to say about it."

That was the slap in the face I needed. "Here's the thing, Mom. You *don't* have a say in it. This is my life. *Mine*. You have absolutely no idea what kind of man Aiden is, what he's done for —" *Nope, not going there.* "I don't recall you saying I turned my back on the family business when I didn't become a pharmacist like Dad."

"Well, no, of course not—"

"I also don't recall Aiden's bar doing poor business before we started seeing each other. Seems to me he was doing just fine." She had nothing to say to that one. "So, here's how this is gonna go." *Who am I right now?* I didn't know and I didn't care. I felt stronger than I ever had. "I'm going to continue dating Aiden, and you're going to stay out of it. If I get hurt, that's on me, but I won't allow you to interfere in something that is possibly the best thing to ever happen to me." I internally grimaced, the truth in that still yet to be determined; although, more and more lately, I wanted it to be true. Especially after last night.

"But let me make something perfectly clear, if you continue to interfere in my love life, you're going to end up pushing me away. I don't want that, and I doubt you do either, but it's inevitable if you don't start respecting my decisions." I recalled Aiden's words from last night. "Could I get hurt? Yeah. But, that's life." I kissed her on the forehead, still fuming but determined to show her I loved her, despite her meddling. "I love you. I just…need some space."

I walked away from my mom, possibly for the first time ever, with an ache in my chest so big it was staggering. My mom had planted enough seeds of doubt to grow a fucking garden. I knew Aiden wasn't using me, at least not in the way she meant. Still, there was a planet-sized crater of fear in my heart that I was nothing more than an experiment. What if we took things further and he found he couldn't do it? Or worse, what if he decided he needed more experience with this newfound side of himself and wanted to test it out with other people? Drake had already proved to me that I was the placeholder, not the permanent choice.

Burke and Levi gave me concerned looks when I came back to the table. I could see Ford and Noah with equally worried expressions from the table next to us, but I shook my head with a sad smile. Knowing me the way they did, they left me alone. When I was ready, I'd tell them what was going on. Right now, I needed to focus on getting the Coral Pointe Inn and Shore Thing Tours more business. There were enough people from out of town who frequented our fairs to warrant setting up shop all weekend. My farce of a love life could wait.

I was exhausted by the time we closed up for the night. The guys had already left, but Sage needed a ride home. His brother-in-law had borrowed his car for the day while theirs was in the shop, and Sage's sister left early to be with the kids. Leaning against the trunk of my car, I watched the reflection of the marina lights dance on the water, heard the faint music coming from SandBar. Closing my eyes, I breathed in the salty air, trying and failing to push the argument with my mom from my brain.

I jumped, the space around me closing in from a warm body, my eyes popping open. "Drake," I hissed, all firmness in my voice nowhere to be found. My hand immediately went to his chest, my pulse jumping from the proximity of him. "What are you doing?"

"You've made your point, Cole. Don't you think you're taking it a bit too far now?" He lifted a hand to my cheek, but it didn't feel the same as it always had.

"What point? What are you talking about?" The cadence of my voice trembled, but I kept my hand firmly in place, not letting him come any closer. Although, I wasn't sure there was room left between us anyway.

"If you were trying to make me jealous, you could've at least gone with a guy who likes dick. I doubt he knows what to do with one of them, never mind two." I caught his hand before it could go anywhere near my junk.

"You need to back up, Drake. I'm serious." *Way to sound strong, dumbass.* "You didn't want me, remember?"

"Maybe I was too hasty." Drake gripped my hip tightly. I shoved him hard, but he only took a small step back. Not enough to clear my confusing thoughts. He brushed his finger down my bottom lip. "I miss this mouth." I hit his hand away in disgust and wiped my mouth with the back of my hand.

"Where's Water Boy? I'm sure he'd be more than willing to let you use his mouth however the fuck you want."

Drake snorted. "Oh, I assure you, he does. Doesn't mean I don't miss yours."

"You're the one who said I wasn't enough. *You're* the one who said my only talent was sucking cock. Or have you forgotten?" Fuck, I couldn't get my words to come out as anything but shaky and weak to save my life, but I absolutely would not cry in front of him. He'd always had a chip on his shoulder, but

in that moment I saw how cruel he'd become.

"We all have our strengths, Cole. Even if that jackass, Rafferty, is suddenly into guys, he's going to get bored. Do you really think he's gonna stick with the first guy he fucks?" He laughed, as if I was too pathetic to see all this on my own. "Hell, he'll be like a kid in a candy store. Coral Pointe is swarming with gay men ready to show Aiden a good time, though god knows why. Except, now you won't just have men to compete with, will you? Think of all the women ready and willing to show him why he should stick with tits and pussy. A veritable smorgasbord of sexual possibilities."

I completely deflated, sick to my stomach as his words hit their intended target. "It's not like that," I said pathetically, too tired to even keep my hand up between us, my confidence fading.

Drake took a step closer and I cringed, surprising even myself. I'd never had that reaction to him being this close before. "Has he even fucked you yet?"

My head shot up, eyes wide.

"Ah, so he doesn't know yet that your technique needs some work." Tears lined my eyes, the heat of embarrassment flooding my cheeks and rushing down my neck. "At least I know where your strengths lie and am willing to overlook the rest."

"Myers, get your fucking hands off him."

I'd never been so relieved to hear Aiden's voice in my life. Instantly, my relief turned to ultimate humiliation. How much of that had Aiden heard?

Drake hung his head back and groaned. "For the love of god, Rafferty. Don't you have a business to run?"

"I said get your fucking hands off him. *Now.*"

I squeezed my eyes shut, willing the tears to cooperate, at least until I could get the hell out of here and in my house. Giving a sidelong glance to Aiden, my breath caught with how beautiful he was. My mom's voice asking me, "Why you?" combined with Drake's eagerness to remind me I wasn't enough—every fucking chance he got—made my knees buckle.

"What's going on?" Sage asked from behind us, pushing my limit of humiliation past the point of too fucking much for one night.

I shoved Drake *hard*, catching him by surprise as he stumbled back. A stupid tear slipped out, sliding down my cheek along with my dignity. Abruptly, I turned, tossing my keys at Sage. "Take my fucking car. I need to be alone."

"Cole…" I heard Sage say, then Aiden shouted my name even louder. I turned and met Aiden's frustrated stare, walking backward and putting my hands up. "Don't follow me. I just…can't right now." My steps were heavy, my vision blurry with tears I frantically wiped away. I kept my feet moving until I was outside Noah's place, pounding on the door.

It took a minute, but the door flew open. Noah's, "What the hell?" dying off as soon as he saw me. "Cole, what's wrong?" He yanked me inside, pulling me into his arms, and like a fool, I just cried. "It's okay, sweetie. I got you." Noah held the back of my head, rubbing a hand up and down my back.

Finally, I pulled away, wiping the last of my tears away. "Fuck, I'm such an ass, huh?"

"For crying?"

Shrugging my shoulders, I looked down at my feet. "That, and everything else."

Noah took my face in his hands, leaning his head down to look in my eyes. "Did Aiden hurt you?"

"No," I rushed out. "This isn't his fault. I doubt he wants to see me again after tonight, though." I put a hand up in front of me. "I just want to go to bed. Can I stay here tonight?"

"Of course, sweetie." Noah was a gentle man with serene gray eyes. His light brown hair was sun kissed with golden highlights. Some would call him a gentle giant because he was the tallest of the group with the biggest heart to match. We all teased him about being the mother hen. Which was exactly why my feet had instinctively taken me to Noah. I needed someone to hold me up while not asking what happened, threatening to break some kneecaps, or trying to make me laugh.

Quickly, he shut his outside and foyer lights off, blanketing the house in darkness.

Without another word, Noah took my hand and guided me to his bedroom. He got the shower going for me, handing me shorts and a T-shirt from his drawer. They were big on me, but they would do. I shut my phone completely off, blocking out the outside world. It felt good to wash the horrible day off my body. Too bad mortification couldn't be washed away, never to replay in my mind again. No such luck.

As I crawled into bed, Noah yanked me down next to him, wrapping his arms around me. "Sleep. Tomorrow, we'll talk, okay?"

I nodded my head against his chest, grateful for how well he knew me. Tomorrow I'd have to deal with it all, but tonight, I just wanted to forget. Forget the radiating anger in Sage's voice, forget the degrading things Drake had said, but most of all, I wanted to forget the pain in Aiden's eyes as I'd walked away.

CHAPTER 13

AIDEN

"What do you mean he's not here. Where is he?" I asked Burke, my patience running thin. It was the last day of the festival and Cole hadn't shown up. I'd waited all night to speak to him, not getting a reply to any of my texts or calls. I was worried sick.

I wasn't supposed to go by the marina last night, but Jesse had forgotten to bring one of the coolers back that we needed this morning. I'd offered to walk back and get it, seeing as how she had several tables she was working and it was almost time for me to call it a night.

That was when I saw them. Drake had Cole backed up against the trunk of his car and my fucking heart sank like a two-ton anchor, dragging me to a stop. For a stupid moment, I'd assumed the worst, until Cole shoved Drake. The asshole hadn't gone far and was back in Cole's face in seconds. I'd taken a few steps closer, every muscle in my body twitching to pound Drake into the concrete. Restraining myself, I'd stayed in the shadows. Cole needed to know he was strong enough to stand up to Drake on his own without me going all caveman.

Anger, the likes of which I'd never felt before, tightened my limbs, my fists squeezed until my fingertips had left marks in the palms of my hands. The vile things Drake had said, the insults, the utter bullshit… I'd watched in horror, realizing too little too late that Cole wasn't standing up for himself. He wasn't saying anything. He'd frozen in place the way he had the night all this had started. Had he believed all that bullshit Drake spat out? I'd been back in fucking Coral Pointe for three years, and in that time, I wasn't exactly fucking the entire female population. For him to think I'd add all the single gay men to my list, like I couldn't keep my dick in my pants…

That's when I'd caught a glimpse of the slight tremble in Cole's bottom lip, heard Drake telling Cole he'd be willing to overlook his bad techniques in bed—and I just snapped.

And, when Cole had walked away and told me not to follow him, my heart cracked a little, doubt sinking back in that maybe he really did think I was using him.

Now he wasn't here, skyrocketing my anger about the whole situation.

"Aiden," Noah said, touching my arm. "He just needed a day to himself. You didn't do anything wrong, but he's…" He looked at the other guys like he wasn't sure what to say.

"He's fucking scared of getting hurt again." Burke crossed his tree trunks for arms over his chest. Maybe that intimidated some people, but I sure as hell wasn't one of them. I appreciated his fierceness in protecting Cole, though. That was something we had in common. "You gonna hurt him, Aiden?"

"What? No!" Jesus Christ, was there anyone in this town who didn't make assumptions about me? *Cole.* At least, I didn't think he did. His assumptions were more about himself. That he wouldn't be enough for someone, me included.

"That's what we thought," Burke added. My shoulders eased, the rage inside me cooling to a simmer. "So, here's what you're gonna do."

I snorted. "You're a bossy fucker, huh?"

"Don't even get us started," Ford chimed in, the other two nodding in agreement.

Burke hiked a thumb over his shoulder. "Someone's gotta rein these jackasses in." Levi opened his mouth to argue, and without even looking, Burke lifted a finger to Levi's lips and shushed him. I had to admit, it was pretty damn funny. "As I was saying. Let Cole have his time alone. He needs it and I don't blame him. *But*…then you need to show him he's wrong. I'm not gonna get all…*profess your love to him or fuck off.* If you truly want to see what's between you two, we're all for it. But if this is something you don't think you can handle—the whispering, the constant coming out…because that'll happen…the negative judgment by way of dirty looks or the positive encouragement by way of butting in your damn business—walk away now."

"No pressure there, huh, Aiden?" Jared slapped me on the back, startling me. With the four men in front of me on the other side of the table, I was relieved to have someone on my side, both figuratively and literally. He casually smiled at Burke, but the squeeze on my shoulder indicated he had my back. Not that I needed it with these guys, but it was good to know.

"You got something to say about it, fisherboy?" Burke asked, a dark brow cocked, his stance widening as if gearing up for a fight—which was just laughable with Jared Boone involved. Jared demonstrated that point with a chuckle.

"Well, let's see…how about not scaring the guy into backing off?" That casual smile stayed plastered on Jared's face. He wasn't much for violence or anger. Hell, he'd perfected the art of pissing people off just by staying calm. Watching Burke lose his cool was one of Jared's greatest pleasures.

"What are you talking about? I told the guy to go after Cole," Burke snapped, waving a hand in my direction.

"Only if Aiden's willing to face all sorts of scary, negative shit, right? How about go after Cole if he can see a future with him? Go after Cole because he thinks he's worth it. Go after him because Aiden's been dealing with gossip and whispers for the past three years and he's still going strong." Jared shrugged a shoulder, his smile expanding. "Something like that." I had to force back a laugh.

Burke looked surprisingly sheepish but quickly schooled his features. "Well, yeah. That too."

"Perfect. So, we're all on the same page." Jared had the balls to wink at Burke, making the big man glower and walk off, muttering something about pain in the ass fisherman and their damn bait. Squeezing my shoulder again, Jared said softly, "You got this," then he walked away.

I took a deep breath, about to go back to my table when Noah caught my arm. "Burke means well. He's just a little rough around the edges. Just know we're all rooting for you. If you can make Cole happy, that's all that matters."

"Thanks. I'll do my best." I meant it. I didn't know where this thing with Cole was going, but friends-with-benefits didn't seem to cover my growing feelings for the guy. If Cole was willing to see where this could go between us, so was I.

COLE

I felt like a coward for skipping out on the last day of the festival, but I'd made sure the guys had enough coverage. That meant sending one of the servers from Oceanside to help out at the table while I summoned my inner college server and waited tables in the restaurant. It wasn't ideal, but it sure as hell kept me busy. So busy, I was dead on my feet by the time I got home. I showered and changed into loose-fitting shorts and a tee, poured myself a glass of cabernet, and stretched out on the couch, ready to put on Lost in Space and get lost in Ignacio Serricchio for an hour or two.

Pounding on my door yanked me out of my escapism, dumping me back into the gloomy reality of my life. I held my breath, hoping whoever it was would go away.

"Cole, I know you're home." Aiden's deep, powerful voice penetrated the wood of the door. "I'll wait out here all night if I have to." Slowly, I crept to the living room window, peaking out at the man standing on my doorstep in the dark, his face lit up by the sensor light. "I'm prepared to spend the night out here. Think the bench is comfortable? Wonder what your neighbors will think when they wake up and find me camping outside your house. Lovers' quarrel?"

"Shit," I whispered. *Stop being a fucking coward.* Pushing my shoulders back, I forced myself to walk to the door, opening it with every intention of telling Aiden it wasn't a good time. He left me no room to even get the words out, crowding me back against the open door. He didn't touch me, didn't trap me in like Drake had, even though every cell in my body screamed for him to.

"I had to see for myself that you're okay." His green eyes flickered as he gazed into mine, his brows drawn together in concern. I felt like a complete asshole. Whatever my insecurities, Aiden didn't deserve to think he'd done something wrong.

"I'm okay," I whispered, my heart skipping a beat as Aiden moved the slightest bit closer, still not touching me.

"Then why aren't you answering my texts or phone calls?" His concern was laced with the slightest hint of hurt…maybe a little bit of anger too.

"Can we not do this in my open doorway?" I took his arm,

pulling him far enough inside so I could close the door. He backed me against the door again, this time with a hand on either side of my head but *still* not touching me. My cock filled in my shorts, the lightweight material doing nothing to hide the fact I was free-balling it.

Aiden glanced down, sucking in a breath from the sight of my shorts tenting. I closed my eyes, my head bouncing back against the wood with a thump.

"Look at me." His voice was demanding, deep and sexy, and I had no choice but to follow the command. "Do you know how many women I've fucked since I came back home?" I glanced away because, no, actually, I did not want to hear about his sexual adventures, thank you very much. Aiden pressed two fingers to my jaw and turned my head until I looked at him again. "Two one-night stands. In three years. And they don't even live in Coral Pointe."

"Why are you telling me this?" I hated the damn tremble I couldn't control.

"'A veritable smorgasbord of sexual possibilities?' Is that really who you think I am?" I had no escape from the wounded look in his eyes, and it hit me all at once that he really had heard every embarrassing thing Drake had said last night.

"No, I don't think that's who you are, but that doesn't mean what he said about me wasn't—*fuck*." I sucked in a breath again, squeezing my eyes shut. Wasn't there a limit to how much embarrassment a person should have to endure in one fucking month? Because I was sure I'd exceeded that limit by leaps and bounds over the last week alone. Not really something I wanted to excel at.

"Wasn't what? A pathetic tactic to try and get you back? A load of shit? Did you forget what happened between us the other night? Because I sure as hell can't. You've been on my mind constantly, Cole." The sound of my name in his raspy baritone was something I'd never get tired of hearing. "When you give yourself over or, fuck, when you give yourself permission to let go and take what you want?" He shook his head. "There's nothing sexier than that." He moved closer still, and I found myself gripping his hips, drawing him against me. We both hissed as our erections rubbed together. "I don't want other people's bullshit between us. I don't want *anything* between us." He snapped the waistband of my shorts and I flinched in anticipation, a rush of air leaving me as my dick grew rock hard.

"*Nghh…*" Articulation was not my strong suit at that moment.

"I'm not some asshole who only takes," Aiden continued. "If I'm with someone, I want all of them, not just the stuff that brings me pleasure. Not just the stuff that brings us *both* pleasure. I want everything. Dates and laughs. Someone I can count on. Are you hearing me?"

"Yes," I whispered, licking my lips.

"I could show you all the ways I've pictured us together, but the truth is, I'm the inexperienced one here." He leaned in, nuzzling into my neck, then whispered in my ear, "I'd much prefer if you took the lead, Cole. Show me what you want."

My fear fucking shattered, every crack flooding with need so staggering my body just took over. Crashing my mouth over his, I pushed my tongue inside that hot, wet haven, wrapping my arms around his neck. Aiden's hands landed on my ass, my body becoming weightless as he lifted me off my feet. I hooked my legs around him, locking my ankles together, rubbing my cock against his stomach as he carried me to my bedroom. I felt frantic to be near him, to feel him with nothing in between us, especially my insecurities.

We neared the bed and I dropped my legs, expecting him to lay me down. Instead he rotated, turning us both around, and sat down, pulling me until I straddled his lap. Squirming against him,

I whimpered, threading my fingers through his hair, tasting every inch of his mouth. His hands traveled up the back of my shirt, his palms leaving a hot trail against my overheated skin. That sinful mouth left mine, his delicious tongue and lips making their way across my jaw to my ear.

"I'm in your capable hands. Take what you want."

The last thread of hesitation disintegrated, the sound torn from my throat—somewhere between a rumbling growl and a belly-deep moan—unrecognizable to my own ears. I ripped my shirt over my head, immediately seizing his and tossing it with mine on the floor. "Naked. I want you naked."

Standing up on shaky legs, I pushed my shorts down, kicking them to the side. My skin felt hot, prickling with awareness and need, his eyes taking in every bare inch of me. I'd usually been one for modesty, but it was thrilling to feel that vulnerable, almost on the edge of too much. I'd never offered myself to anyone the way I was offering myself to him right now.

Aiden's eyes darkened, his tongue snaking out to wet his lips. "Jesus Christ, Cole. I've never seen anyone sexier."

"You're overdressed," I pointed out, reveling in the way he was staring at me in awe.

Aiden stood in front of me, his eyes locked on mine. He kicked off his sneakers, opened his jeans, and pushed them down along with his black boxer briefs. Then he sat down on the edge of the bed, holding my gaze, pulling the last of his clothes off until he was as naked as I was. There was no denying how turned on he was, his thick, veiny cock standing tall and proud…enticing.

"Come here," he said, holding his arms out to me.

I didn't hesitate, climbing back into his lap, my eyes crossing as a groan rolled out from the delicious slide of our cocks. I wrapped around him while my brain tried to wrap around the fact that this was Aiden holding me…Aiden whose fingers traced the length of my spine. Aiden, the sexy man I'd known for years but now would know in a way I never dreamed possible.

Using the weight of my body, my knees on the mattress, I pushed forward. Aiden's back landed on the bed with me on top of him. I kissed my way down to his chest, tongue and teeth working each of his nipples into a peak. He arched his back, pushing his fingers through my hair and holding on. *Sensitive nipples...noted.* I feasted on every inch of his torso—his dusting of chest hair that felt slightly coarse on my tongue, discovering he was a little ticklish by his ribs, the hills and valleys of his abs. Pushing my nose into the seam where his thigh met his groin, his cock brushed against the side of my cheek and I breathed in. His masculine scent would be embedded in my memory for years to come.

Instinctively, I snaked my tongue out, sliding it up the side of his cock. The deep groan he let out was all the confirmation I needed. *This*, I was good at. Slowly, I took the mushroom-shaped tip in my mouth, his flavor exploding on my tongue. Aiden babbled out something I couldn't quite understand because I was lost in the feel of him in my mouth.

"W-wait…wait…" Aiden's words broke through my muddled brain, and I immediately pulled off, wiping my mouth with the back of my hand to hide the mortification flaming my cheeks.

It's too much for him. I can't fault him for—

Strong hands gripped me under my arms, tossing me up into the middle of bed as if I weighed next to nothing. It took me a second to catch up, to realize Aiden was climbing over me, letting his full weight push me into the mattress as he settled between my legs. "Not that I wasn't loving your mouth on me, but tonight's about you. I want to know what you like, how *you* taste." I was pretty sure I'd just swallowed loud enough for him to hear. "I've never sucked a dick before, but I'm a fast learner." He grinned, waggling his eyebrows then snagged my bottom lip with his teeth, tugging gently. "You okay with that?"

I managed a high-pitched hum and a desperate nod of my head.

"Good, because I expect you to be really vocal." He slid his body down mine, his mouth finding my nipple, teeth grazing the sensitive skin. I pushed my head back into the mattress and moaned, not even to follow his command but because I couldn't have stopped it if I tried. Aiden took his time, his tongue tracing my skin until there wasn't a single spot on my torso he hadn't tasted. His hot breath on my heat-damp skin sent a shiver down my spine.

My eyes shot open when Aiden's warm hand wrapped around my cock. I stared open-mouthed down the length of my body, trembled when his grip tightened on a downward stroke. Aiden held my cock up, his mouth above the head, and let a line of spit fall, immediately catching it on the tip of my cock to use as lube.

"Oh fuck," I hissed out, my thighs falling open to the bed.

"You like that?" He did it a few more times after my moan of approval, rubbing his thumb under the sensitive ridge.

"Yes, I like that. Do it with your…" The words got stuck in my throat. I couldn't tell Aiden to do what I wanted. Not when he'd never done that before.

Aiden squeezed my cock, his other hand tugging on my balls. "Tell me." I screwed my eyes shut, my grip on the sheets tight enough to rip right through them. "Look at me." I forced myself to peel my eyes open and meet his. "Whatever it is, I'll do it, but I want to hear you say the words." He swiped his thumb over my slit and I arched my back and cursed.

"Do it with your tongue. I want your mouth on my cock." *Holy shit! Did I really just say that out loud?* "Fuck! Oh my god!" *Yes, yes you did.* And holy fuck did he oblige.

Aiden's tongue flicked back and forth over that sensitive spot under the purple head of my dick, every nerve ending fucking singing. I grabbed his hair, my eyes latched on him, memorizing —so I'd have it for the rest of my life—that moment when he slipped the head of my cock into his mouth for the first time.

"Fuck," I sighed. This had to be Heaven.

CHAPTER 14

AIDEN

I had a dick in my mouth for the first time.

Cole's long, hard dick.

In my mouth.

And I fucking *loved* it.

His skin was salty, silky as I slid my mouth down a bit farther. I didn't want to go too far. I had no idea where my gag reflex was, but I sure as hell wasn't letting that happen the first time I had a self-conscious Cole's dick in my mouth.

Determined to show him I was really fucking into this, I managed to find some kind of rhythm with my mouth and fist. I was lucky I didn't come just hearing him tell me he wanted my mouth on his cock. Damn, that was so sexy. He had no idea how sexy he was.

Desperate little sounds alerted me to the fact he was getting closer and closer to orgasm. His hands gripped tightly in my hair, the sting on my scalp a pleasurable pain. The gentle pump of his hips fell into tempo with my mouth and hand, punctuated by high-pitched noises that went straight to my cock. I would've let him thrust harder, take what he needed from my willing mouth to make him blow.

When I heard my name carried out of his mouth on a moan, I knew he was trying to warn me he was about to come—and I didn't care. It was a very real possibility I'd make a mess of both of us and choke. I didn't care about that either. Fuck, I loved when sex was messy and raw and demanding.

Cole's back arched off the bed, grunting his release as it pumped out of his cock and into my mouth, hot and sticky. I'd said I wanted to hear him, and *fuck*…it was the best sound in the world. I sucked every last drop from him, managing to swallow some while the rest dripped out the corners of my mouth. When his body went limp on the bed, I let his slick cock fall from my mouth, rose up on my knees over him, and fisted my own dick. It didn't take long for my head to throw back on a shout, come landing on Cole's abs as my body shook and my muscles went weak.

I landed with a bounce on the mattress next to Cole, grinning from ear to ear as I tried to catch my breath. Turning my head on the pillow, I caught him staring at me, a picture of awe and satisfaction. I held my breath, waiting for him to say something, but when his gorgeous face split into a gleaming smile, my breath left me in a *whoosh*. He was so beautiful. I'd never thought that about a guy before, but there it was. Cole Sullivan was the most beautiful man I'd ever seen, and in the afterglow of sex? He took my breath away.

Cole grabbed some tissues off the nightstand and wiped us both off, tossing them on the floor. "I have no words…" he said, his hand landing on my chest as he rolled toward me, fingers playing over my skin and through my chest hair. He leaned his other elbow on the mattress, cradling his head in his hand.

"That good or that bad?" I teased.

Cole smacked me on the chest, right over my left nipple. "What do you think?"

"I think I just came so hard I lost brain cells."

He twirled his forefinger in a pattern on my chest, around one nipple, across to the other. If my body was what it once was, I'd be ready to go again for another round. No such luck, even with the valiant effort made by my dick at a twitching attempt.

"You didn't let me return the favor," he said softly, peeking sidelong glances up into my eyes then back down to follow the path of his finger.

I had to tread carefully. "There was no favor to return. I did that as much for me as I did for you." I brushed my fingers through his soft, chestnut hair. "There's no quid pro quo here. I sucked your cock because I wanted to, not because I expected something in return." Never in my life did I think that sentence would ever leave my mouth, but I meant every word.

"You really mean that, don't you?"

"Yeah, I do."

The smile I was rewarded was so worth proving to Cole that he was more than just an available mouth. That asshole had really done a number on him.

"I'm sorry about last night."

"What are you sorry for?"

Cole shrugged and sighed, falling onto his back as he stared up at the ceiling and pushed his hand into his hair. "I shouldn't have left you there like that. You didn't deserve it."

I could've backed off, told him it was okay, but I was going for utter honesty with him, wasn't I? I leaned up on my forearm. If I'd learned anything about Cole in the last month, it was that I needed him to look at me, to see in my eyes that I meant what I was saying. "I won't lie and say it didn't suck. I figured out pretty quickly that you probably hadn't gone home. I didn't know which guy's house you ended up at, but yeah, it kind of stung. I'm not sure I realized until that moment that I wanted to be the person you turn to or, at least, one of them. Maybe one day you'll trust me enough to do that.

"Having said that, you don't need to apologize, either. Whatever's happening between us, I think it took us both by surprise."

"That's an understatement." He let go of his hair and cupped my cheek, his thumb brushing back and forth against my skin. "You're right. I'm used to turning to one or all of the guys when I'm upset, but you have to know how much you've been there for me over the last month. Even before all this"—he waved a hand between us—"you were becoming someone I looked for when things went to shit. I still do. I was just so embarrassed you'd heard all that. The worst part was, in my fucked-up state of humiliation, I didn't defend you when you have done nothing but defend me since this whole thing started."

"You stood up to my pop. That took guts." I skated my hand across his stomach, grasping his waist. "Not to mention it was sexy as hell."

"Yeah?" he breathed out, pulling my arm until I rolled on top of him.

"Hell yeah." I nodded, capturing his mouth, my body apparently having enough down time judging by how my cock filled against his stomach.

He reached in the drawer by the bed, pulling out a bottle of lube. Hand slick, he stroked us together until we both emptied onto his chest, trembling and sweaty.

After cleaning up, he asked me to stay, which I had a sneaking suspicion also took guts. Little did he know, I had no intention of leaving.

I spent the next several nights at Cole's. Of course, that only amped everyone's interest, as if my car being in front of his house every night was big news. Didn't make much sense considering Cole and I, for all intents and purposes, were in a relationship. We hadn't discussed the validity of what we were doing, but that didn't change how my feelings for him were morphing into something almost overwhelming. Nights were spent in his bed, learning each other's bodies with mouths and hands. I still wouldn't let him suck me off, determined to prove Drake wrong. I sure as hell amped up my cocksucking abilities, though. There was nothing better than making Cole come so hard, his muscles locked up tight as he screamed my name.

"Wow, I can almost see the dirty thoughts bouncing off every wall of your brain." Jared raised an eyebrow and took a slow sip of his beer. "I feel like I need a cigarette just being near you."

I snorted, continuing my task of drying off the glass in my hand. Setting it down, I moved closer to him, glancing around as I lowered my voice. "Is it crazy to be so happy from something that started as a lie?"

"From where I'm sitting, that goofy smile on your face sure as hell ain't fake." He popped a fry in his mouth. "So, when are you both gonna wake up and admit it's not?"

I rubbed the back of my neck, that question was one I had asked myself several times over the last week. "Shit, I don't know. I'm sort of just following his lead. Trying not to overwhelm him." Leaning my weight on the bar in front of Jared, I admitted, "Being attracted to a guy never crossed my mind before, or so I thought."

"What do you mean?"

"I notice all sorts of shit about people who come in here. Hear all the gossip, know what someone usually orders, that kind of thing. But with Cole…" I shook my head, somewhere between awe and *What took me so long?* "My attention would be on him the second he'd walk in. At first I thought it was just habit, then I figured it was because I knew Drake was gonna stand him up again and again and I felt bad for him, but…" I exhaled long and slow, pulling Cole's face up in my mind. "I don't know. I'd get caught in the way he smiled or laughed at something. I think I'd made it my mission to make him laugh. And on the nights Drake would be in here with some other guy, I physically had to force myself to stay out of it. You know me. I don't get involved in other people's shit but, man, did I jump right in the middle of Cole's."

"You sure did. Just got on that platform and dove headfirst into that pool. Lucky for you, I think you've managed to create a splash without belly flopping." Jared chuckled then took a bite of his BLT wrap.

"I think I've done a pretty good job so far, but I don't know. His views on what relationships should be are so skewed. Obviously, I know why. It's just hard to see someone as smart and as kind and as gorgeous as Cole let a man like that asshole shit on his worth. He deserves so much more than that."

"Then show him. Prove him wrong."

"I shoulda thought of that." The answer had been staring me in the face and somehow I'd missed it. I looked up what I needed on my phone, grinning like a fucking loon the whole time when I made the call. "Hey, Lyle, can you make a delivery for me? It's going to Coral Pointe Inn." Jared nodded his approval, giving me a thumbs up.

I couldn't brush this off anymore as something not real, when all I wanted to do was make Cole happy. I wished I could see his face when the delivery was made, because that was the reward. Not mind-blowing sex—which so far, *holy hell*—or wanting something in return, except to know he was feeling what I was feeling. That I wasn't alone in this.

There was no point going back through the last month, trying to figure out where things had changed. It didn't matter. All that mattered was Cole made me feel things I hadn't felt in years. I wasn't even sure I'd ever felt them with Sasha.

I wanted to take care of him, but there was a belly-deep need to have him be there for me, too. God knew, I was tired of going it alone. Sure, I had Jared, Sage, and Billy, but it wasn't the same as what was growing between me and Cole. It had caught me by surprise, but in the best possible way.

My phone rang in my pocket an hour later, Cole's name lighting up the screen. "Hey there." I gave Jesse a signal and pointed to my office, closing myself in so I could give Cole my full attention without the beat of steel drums in my ears.

"Aiden, these are… They're absolutely beautiful." I could hear the smile in his voice. It would have to be enough for now.

"Coral's Florals has some pretty nice arrangements." I dropped down in my chair and threw my feet up on my desk, crossing my ankles. I was damn proud of myself, but making Cole happy was becoming my favorite thing.

"They do, but that's not what I meant." He paused for a few beats and I held my breath. "I've never been sent flowers before." His voice was so soft, I was grateful to be in my quiet office.

"Then I'm glad I was the first. You know what they say about your first." I wiggled my eyebrows, even though he couldn't see me.

Cole's laugh was loud through the speaker. "I'm glad you were, too."

"So, what about the question on the card? Are you free tomorrow afternoon? I have to cover the bar at six, but I thought maybe we could spend some time together." *Out of the bedroom.* It was getting to the point where I wanted him all the damn time, making it even more crucial to prove that wasn't all I was after. Luckily, I already knew he had tomorrow off. Perfect timing.

"What did you have in mind?"

"It's a surprise." *Note to self...figure out where to take him.* I hadn't exactly thought this through all the way, but there had to be something we could do that didn't involve staying home.

"Sounds good." There was a shuffling on the other end, followed by, "Sorry, Aiden, but I have to go. One of the employees needs me up front. I'll see you tomorrow?"

"Tomorrow." I ended the call, a cheesy grin on my face.

Standing up from my chair, I headed back out into the bar, dialing Sage's number as I went.

"Hey, cuz. To what do I owe the pleasure? Wait, hold on a sec…" Something brushed over the speaker of the phone on his end, his voice slightly muffled. "Kenneth, I'm sorry she dumped you, truly, but table five needs bread. No, I don't know what she meant by that." Pause. "I'm sure you're a stallion." Another pause. "It happens to the best of us." Pause with Sage's muffled laugh into the phone. "Of course, it does. We're only human. But do you know what shouldn't get hard, Kenneth? Bread. That's right. Run along. She didn't deserve you. More fish in the sea and all that." Sage exhaled into the receiver. "Aiden, what is it about me that screams sex therapist or *knows how to pleasure a woman*? For fuck's sake! The last time I came in contact with a vagina I was being born!"

I busted out a laugh, hanging my head. "If it's any consolation, I don't need any help in that department."

"I'm not sure whether to be proud or grossed out."

"Fair enough. Actually, I was calling for advice, though."

"I'll do my best. What's up?"

"I need an idea for a late-afternoon date."

"With Cole?" There was no mistaking the *tread lightly* tone in that question.

"Of course, with Cole. What kind of question is that?" It was one thing having to convince Cole I was serious, but having to prove it to everyone else was really starting to get on my fucking nerves.

"Okay, okay. Simmer down, lover boy. I'm just making sure. So, here's what you're gonna do..." Sage hashed out his plan to me, which I admit, was kind of perfect.

I couldn't help the smile I had on my face. It had been a long time since I'd felt that things in my life were falling into place. I glanced around the busy bar, giddiness washing over me to see people enjoying themselves, drinking beer I'd made, eating at tables I'd help put together.

Then there was Cole. He was a completely unexpected—yet absolutely welcomed—facet of my life now. I'd loved this bar since the day I'd opened the doors. I'd never felt like a workaholic before. Thinking about spending time with Cole shifted something inside me. I still loved spending my days here, but now I had something else to look forward to.

"Hey, Aiden? Can you bring this salad to Edna?" Jesse asked, her other hand balancing a full tray on her shoulder. "Fair warning, she's feisty today. Apparently, there was too much chicken in her chicken Caesar salad. God forbid she just push aside what she doesn't want. Not like we can do anything with it but throw it out anyway." She shook her head in derision, rolling her eyes.

"Great," I snorted. "Yeah, I got it." I took the salad from her and carried it across the bar to a table by the wall where Edna sat with her sister Peggy. "Hey there, Edna. Here's your salad." No way in hell I was comping her bill for giving her *too* much food. Seeing that Peggy had already been served, I asked, "Can I get you ladies anything else?"

Edna sighed, making sure I knew the whole thing was an inconvenience. "That'll be all for now, I suppose."

I plastered a big fucking smile on my face. "Great! Enjoy."

Apparently, when I turned around to walk away was when she

thought it was a good time to take aim. Nothing like attacking from behind. "It's just such a disgrace what he's done to his father. Poor Jim was all alone when he had that scare the other day."

Scare? The other day meaning the festival? But he wasn't alone then… My spine stiffened as I slowly turned around, my nostrils flaring but chin held high. "Is there something you'd like to say to me, Edna?"

For a second, she looked caught off guard, but it didn't take long for her self-righteous nose to point upward. "I'm just not sure how you can live with the fact you turned your back on your family. And to think, Jim was staring at the pearly gates on Wednesday and now here you are. Smiling as if you haven't a care in the world. 'Course, it's none of my business how you choose to live your life."

My pulse pounded in my ears as each and every thing she'd said filtered through my brain. *Staring at the pearly gates? Why didn't anyone call me?* Deep in my gut, I knew he had to be okay or Sage would've said something. I couldn't do this here in front of her…in front of everyone. Funny how I was such a fucking disappointment, yet she continued to be a patron in my traitorous bar.

I forced myself to keep a shuttered expression. No way in hell I'd let her know how she'd just destroyed the good day I was having. "You're right, Edna. It's none of your business. Enjoy your lunch, ladies."

I heard Edna and Peggy gasp as I walked away, not shocked by "The nerve of that boy!" It was always my fault. That was never going to change, was it?

Jesse gave me an apologetic look, mouthing *I'm sorry* to me. I waved her off as if it didn't matter, but no sooner had I closed myself off in my office, I called Billy. "What happened to my pop the other day?"

"Hello to you, too, Aiden. So nice to hear from you. Lovely

weather we're having, isn't it?" Her tone was dry, dripping with sarcasm I had no patience for.

"Billy, cut the shit and tell me what's going on."

"What are you talking about? You were there at the festival and saw what I saw."

"Not at the festival. Something happened on Wednesday, which Edna Lawry was kind enough to point out in the snidest possible way."

"Aiden, I honestly have no idea." Billy's voice softened, concern obvious in her voice. "I didn't hear anything about Wednesday. What did Edna say?"

"To sum up? I'm a shit son for not being there when he was *staring at the pearly gates* on Wednesday." I paced my small office, hands trembling from anger…but mostly fear.

"That vile woman needs a hobby. Or to get laid…" She made gagging noise into the phone. "Ew…that was a gross thought."

Huffing out a laugh, I slumped down into my chair. "So, you really had no idea? Because you didn't mention any of this happening before."

"I know and that was wrong. I'm sorry. He kept insisting he was alright and it was just heartburn. But I swear, I don't know anything about Wednesday."

My anger deflated. It was shitty to keep putting her in the middle of the drama. It wasn't her place to be his fucking babysitter, either. If he would just let her take over the damn business… "It's okay. I get it. You're in a tough spot. Thanks for everything, Billy."

"Anytime, Aiden."

I hit Pop's contact next, holding my breath until he answered. I'd never been on the phone so much in my life. "Rafferty's." He had caller ID—I knew it; he knew it—yet, he still answered the phone like I was nothing more than a customer.

If that was the game he wanted to play, so be it. No niceties required. "When were you going to tell me or, hell…Billy, about what happened on Wednesday?"

"Nothin' to tell."

"Is that why Edna Lawry claims you were on death's door?"

"That woman is insufferable," he grumbled.

"Agreed. Still doesn't tell me where she got the idea from. There must be some truth to it." Jesus, every fucking thing was like pulling teeth with him. These were the days I missed my mom with a bone-deep sadness. She'd have stopped this shit from happening years ago.

"She came in the other day wanting to hang some flyers for a knitting club or some nonsense, I had heartburn, the end."

"Pop…"

"What's this I hear about you kissing the gates of Heaven on Wednesday?" Billy shouted in the background. I was surprised it had taken her that long to get there.

"Oh, for the love of… Y'all need to stop listening to Edna Lawry, for Christ's sake. I don't have time for this. I have a *business* to run."

Couldn't let one dig get by, could ya, Pop?

"If you think we're done talking, old man, you're crazy," Billy snapped, and I laughed, in spite of the mood I was in. The phone shuffled, Pop grumbling words I couldn't make out. "Gimme that," she said to him. "Aiden, I got it from here. This man is gettin' a piece of my mind."

"Over my dead—"

"Don't you say it, Uncle Jim! This isn't a joke." She was still yelling at him when the call disconnected. I didn't know whether to be grateful or pissed off, but terrified? Yeah, that emotion came through loud and clear.

CHAPTER 15

COLE

"So, where are you taking me?" I hadn't gone on a date in longer than I could remember. I couldn't even count the meetups with Drake at SandBar because they were nothing more than a way to humor me before going back to my place. Majority of the time, I'd paid even though he'd asked me to meet him. And to think, all that time I'd settled for being treated that way, allowing Drake to treat me like nothing more than a booty call. Comparing Aiden to Drake was like comparing a five-course meal to a five-dollar fast food deal, and I definitely knew which one I wanted to eat.

Aiden surprised me, leaning across the console of his car to kiss me. Yeah, it was safe to say I was rusty at dating. "You'll see." He pulled onto the road, reaching his hand over and linking it with mine on my thigh. "This okay?"

I curled my fingers around his hand, my belly fluttering with a swarm of butterflies. "Yeah." It was *really* okay—so okay I was terrified to get used to it. I was happier than I had been in years. When I'd gotten the flowers at the inn the day before, shocked wasn't even a big enough word to describe how I'd felt. I'd stared at them all day as they sat on my desk, most likely with a goofy smile on my face. So fucking worth Burke's and Levi's teasing.

We pulled into the parking lot next to a quiet section of the beach, away from Aiden's crowded bar and most tourists. There were a few couples and families, but there was more room to spread out. Not exactly where I'd expected him to bring me, but I didn't care. Spending time with him was the only thing that mattered.

"I didn't bring a suit or anything. Sadly, I think they frown upon skinny dipping." I pushed out my bottom lip in a teasing pout.

Aiden's eyes darkened, perusing my body until my skin prickled with goosebumps and my mouth ran dry. "Shame." He pulled me in for another kiss and I melted into it with a sigh. He tasted like mint with an unexpected hint of urgency, the combo shooting straight to my dick. "As much as I love you naked, I've only got a couple of hours. The date will have to do for now."

The only three words I caught out of that entire sentence—*I love you*—played in loops in my head. In the context he'd used them, it was the same as saying he loved ice cream or Sunday night football. Yet, I singled them out; the realization that I wanted them to mean something more was staggering. I was beginning to understand there was a reason for that. A reason I wasn't yet ready to completely own.

My habit of getting more attached than the other person stood in my way like a roadblock. Taking the logical route around that possible heartache seemed the smarter choice.

Maybe I wasn't as smart as I thought I was.

I wanted to jump that hurdle like I was in the fucking Olympics, except instead of the gold medal, Aiden would be my reward. *My kind, caring, muscular, sinfully sexy reward.*

"What?" Aiden asked with a laugh.

"What?" *Yep, I just said that last part out loud.* "Should we get out of the car?" *Smooth change of subject.* Jesus, what this man did to me.

"Yeah," he said with another chuckle. "Let's go. I have to get some things out of the trunk." Aiden kissed the back of my hand before letting it go to get out of the car. I met him by the trunk, my eyes landing on the wicker basket in the back.

"A picnic?"

"Perfect day for it, don't you think?" Aiden draped a blue and white plaid blanket over his arm then lifted the basket out, shutting the trunk with his other hand.

"It's a gorgeous day for it." I turned toward the beach path, my hand tingling when Aiden took it in his. Looking down at our joined hands, my heart skipped a beat, and I sucked in a breath. Glancing up into Aiden's eyes, I caught the apprehension in them. Not gonna lie, it was good to see I wasn't the only one who was nervous.

He had no idea of the impact just that simple act of holding my hand in public had on me. I squeezed his even tighter, sliding my other hand up to his bicep. If this man—this gorgeous, sweet, brave man—was willing to own what we were, you can bet your ass I was going to hold on with both hands. Literally. Even though I wasn't exactly sure *what* we were, it felt a lot like a genuine relationship. My track record in the world of love wasn't great, but I was pretty sure we'd abandoned the fake part of our relationship almost as soon as it had started.

Reluctantly, I let go of Aiden so he could spread the blanket out on the sand. We both kicked off our shoes and sat down, and Aiden started emptying the basket. The man had come prepared—and it looked like he'd made a stop by Bluefin before picking me up.

"Coconut shrimp…" he said, setting the container down.

"My favorite."

A sexy smirk curled his lips. "I know." He took another container out. "Crab cakes…"

"Your favorite." I laughed when Aiden gave me a shocked smile. "You're not the only one who pays attention." I'd gotten used to seeing several emotions play out on Aiden's face over the last month and a half. Shyness wasn't one of them. It felt like a victory to see his vulnerability.

"Bacon-wrapped scallops because bacon. And, lastly, crab salad on cucumber rounds. Sage's favorite because…Sage." Aiden rolled his eyes. "He said this wasn't ideal date food, but since we're both eating it, we'll cancel each other out."

When he kissed me again…

I couldn't wait.

"Sounds good to me."

"Oh! I almost forgot…pinot grigio. That one you always have in your fridge." He opened the plastic container and poured me a cup. Was it stupid to love that he knew what kind of wine I had in my fridge?

"Aiden, this is amazing. Thank you."

Aiden shrugged, and again, I was privy to the honest vulnerability in his eyes. "It's just as much for me as it is for you. I really like spending time with you."

"I like spending time with you, too." Boy, did I ever. There wasn't a minute that went by that he wasn't on my mind.

We sat there and got to know even more about each other. Aiden made me laugh with shenanigans he and Billy had gotten into when they were younger. She was closer in age to Aiden than Sage. His face softened when he spoke of his mom. I remembered her from town festivals and when my mom would have the committee over for meetings. She'd always been pretty quiet, but when she talked, they listened. It was obvious who Aiden got his patient nature and quiet strength from.

Aiden leaned back on his hands and hung his head back. "My pop had another episode on Wednesday."

"What? Is he okay?"

I gripped his thigh when a watery gaze landed on me. Not a single tear fell, yet I felt the pain Aiden was going through as if it were my own. Aiden huffed humorously. "He still insists it's just heartburn." Shaking his head, his bottom lip caught between his teeth, he stared off at the ocean. "There isn't a damn day that goes by that I'm not terrified something will happen to him. That we haven't resolved anything, haven't mended our relationship, and by then, it'll be too late.

"As if that wouldn't be devastating enough, some people in this town would make it their life's mission to make sure I never forgot that." He sat up with his legs pulled to his chest and crossed at the ankles, his forearms resting on his spread knees, but the tension in his shoulders belied the casual position.

"Then I'd make it my life's mission to shut them the hell up. So would Sage and Billy and Jared and the guys." I slid closer to him, taking one of his hands in mine. "But I'm sure it won't come to that, okay? Screw the judgmental assholes in this town. Just keep doing what you're doing. You'll know deep down you did everything you could to fix things with him."

His thumb brushed back and forth over the back of my hand. "Sorry I brought the mood down."

"I'm not. Aiden, I want you to be able to come to me, too. This isn't a one-way street, remember? If I'm with someone, I want all of them, just like you do. I've never had that, but you make me want things I've never had before." I couldn't believe I'd said that, yet there wasn't a single part of me that wished I hadn't.

He leaned his forehead against mine, kissed me softly. I soaked him in like a ray of sunlight. That's what he'd become to me, ever since the beginning of all this. My light in the darkness. I was determined to be that for him, too.

By the time Aiden dropped me off at my house, my emotions were all over the damn place. On one hand, I'd had so much fun with him, and all we'd done was talk. Well, and kissed. A lot. Turns out, public displays of affection didn't completely turn me off after all. My comfort level with him didn't change whether we were inside or outside the bedroom. I felt closer to him than I ever had.

On the other hand, hearing him talk about missing his mom and the rough relationship he had with his dad made me realize I'd been upset with my mom for long enough. To her credit, she'd given me space for an entire week. We needed to talk about boundaries, though, if we wanted a good relationship again. That meant her not only accepting whatever was happening between me and Aiden, but also respecting it.

I found myself on my parents' doorstep around dinnertime, which was a *total* coincidence. Okay, sue me if I knew it was Saturday and that meant spaghetti and meatballs with homemade sauce. Raising my hand to the door, I was about to knock when it was yanked open.

"Cole! Oh, honey, I'm so happy you're here!" My mom pulled me into a warm hug, and I Olaf'ed the hell out of it.

She'd crossed the line before in the past, but this was the first time I'd stuck to my guns and kept my distance. It hit me suddenly that nothing she'd done in the past had bothered me as much as her skepticism and judgment toward Aiden. Hell, I'd never even said anything when she would talk badly about Drake—I couldn't argue with the truth—but Aiden was off limits.

"Hey, Mom." I sucked in a gasping breath. "Mom, you can let go now. You know, breathing is important."

"Helen, let Cole in the door, sweetheart." My dad—the Switzerland of our family dynamic—pulled my mom off me and tucked her into his arms in one smooth move. The man was good. He was also the reason I hadn't gone insane from my mom's helicopter parenting over the years.

The table was set for two, but my mom quickly set out another plate, silverware, and wine glass. I sat down and breathed in the familiar scents of my parents' home, smelled the sauce cooking on the stove, heard the familiar sound of seagulls through the open window, carried on a late-spring breeze. It sounded so stupid to say I missed it after only a week, but the thought that Aiden had gone without something like this with his dad for years made me thankful for what I had.

Of course, it didn't take my mom long after we began eating to shift the conversation. She was nothing if not persistent.

"So, how are things with you and Aiden?" She pushed a meatball around her plate, took a sip of her wine. Anything to avoid eye contact with me. Too bad I didn't need to see her eyes to know they were still full of skepticism.

"Things are really great. He's amazing."

She huffed and immediately my back went up. "You know, his daddy had a scare the other day. Of course, he was all alone."

"Helen…" Dad warned.

"What? He did." Shrugging her shoulders innocently, she took a small bite of spaghetti.

I sighed, letting my fork clank on the plate, and sat back in my chair. "Yes, I know he did, Mom. So does Aiden. And no, his dad wasn't alone, hence the overworked gossip mill. Of course, Aiden had to find out through the toxic grapevine because his dad is a stubborn ass."

"Cole! What a thing to say about someone! I raised you better."

I snorted. "Yeah, well, I have a feeling Grandma raised you better, too." My hands were shaking. I'd never spoken to her like that before, and I didn't want to fight with her again, but enough was enough.

When Dad rolled his lips in, trying to hold in a chuckle, my shoulders eased a bit.

"What are you laughing at?" she admonished, giving my dad the stink eye.

"Helen, you have to admit, Cole has a point." He rolled up his napkin and tossed it on the table. "Aiden is a good man. I don't know what you have against him. Anyone with eyes can see he cares about Jim. Hell, he sells Jim's beer at his bar faithfully, just to support Rafferty's."

"If he's such a 'good man,' why did I have to hear from someone else that Cole's dating him? How long did Aiden make him his dirty little secret? There has to be some reason why Cole came to dinner, at this very table, and didn't bother to tell us he was with Aiden. The whole thing came out of the blue. That man saw an opportunity and he pounced. That's how."

"Oh my god, Mom, enough!" I pushed my chair back and stood up, pacing the kitchen. "You want to know the truth? Aiden said he was my boyfriend because Drake was humiliating the hell out of me in the middle of SandBar! No, he wasn't my boyfriend at the time, but he—a man who thought he was straight as an arrow—threw himself to the wolves and took the brunt of all these goddamn rumors. You know why? Because what difference would one more rumor make? Everyone in this town loves to make him the bad guy, anyway. He did it to help *me*, not to double his damn profits."

"I knew it! I knew it couldn't be true!"

I shot her a look that made her shrink down in her chair. "Maybe it didn't start out that way, but it sure as hell is true now. We haven't put a label on it yet, but things have changed. He makes me happier than I've ever been. Why isn't that enough for you?"

"Relationships can't start on lies, Cole."

"But they can start when my mother pimps me out in a ridiculous kissing booth? They can start when my mother is willing to set me up with men she doesn't even know?" I laced my fingers together, cradling the back of my head, still pacing the small room. Abruptly, I stopped and met her eyes, dropping my clenched hands to my sides. "You know what, Mom? Aiden may have done me the favor of pretending to be my boyfriend so I could move on from Drake, but I was more than willing to keep up the charade just to get you off my back."

Her eyes went wide and she sucked in a breath. "Cole…"

"No. I came here tonight to clear the air, but it's impossible to do with your judgmental gossip pollution. I love you, Mom, with all my heart, but things have to change. I see Aiden's heart breaking every time his dad rejects him, every time something reminds him of his mom and what he lost, *every…single…time* someone accuses him of letting his family down. I know how lucky I am to have you and Dad. I even know you think you're helping…that what you're doing comes from a place of love. Well, that's not how love works.

"I've been in a relationship where I said nothing and continued to let someone walk all over me, even though I knew how toxic it was. I'm telling you right now, I won't shut my mouth while you talk badly about Aiden." My breath trembled and my heart raced, but this was worth standing up for. Aiden was worth standing up for. "Because he's the one who's proven to me how love works."

Holy shit, it hit me like a tidal wave. I knew how love worked because I was falling so hard for Aiden I couldn't breathe. The sheer force of it overwhelmed me.

I crossed the kitchen, struck by the tears in my mom's eyes. Kissing the top of her head, I said softly, "I need you to think about everything I said. Aiden is in my life now, whether you like it or not. If you want things with us to get better, you need to accept that. And, if things don't work out between me and Aiden" —I rubbed a hand over my aching heart from just the thought— "that's between us."

I turned away, gripping my dad's shoulder as he gave me a sympathetic smile, but I knew from the nod of his head, he was proud of me for finally standing up for myself. "I'm gonna go," I said to both of them. "I really hope you think about what I said."

My emotions were still all over the place a few hours later when I'd sent out the image of the Bat-Signal. The guys and I had adopted using the cheesy yet effective emblem several years ago. I knew some of the guys, if not all provided they were free, would show up when I needed them, no questions asked.

"Whose ass do I have to kick?" Burke growled the second I opened the door.

"Um…my mom's?"

Ford laughed, pushing past Burke into my house, patting him on the chest on his way by. "Good luck with that one, buddy."

"Well shit. I was hoping it would be Drakeula's." Burke stomped into the kitchen and helped himself to the beer in my fridge.

"You don't need my permission to do that. Have at it." I slumped down into a chair at the table, glancing toward the door as Levi and Noah came in. "Wow. The gang's all here. I feel so honored."

"You should. I was this close"—Ford held his thumb and fore-finger half an inch apart—"to hooking up with a gorgeous redhead on Tinder. You're welcome for choosing you over boobs."

"I'm touched."

"Yeah, well, you know what won't be touched?" Ford's eyes went wide as he threw his hands in the air. "Boobs!"

"Not by you, they won't," Burke ragged to which Ford responded with his middle finger.

"How do all conversations lead back to Ford's sex life?" Levi grumbled, looking uncomfortable. I was beginning to see something I was sure no one else did but, man, would I have to tread lightly with this one.

Ford hopped up on my counter and wiggled his eyebrows. "Because I'm the only one gettin' any."

"Incorrect, sir," I said with a shit-eating grin, and all four heads jerked in my direction.

"Oh *ho*!" Ford clapped his hands together. "Someone's gettin' served by the bartender!"

I barked out a laugh, surprised I even had any to release after the night I'd had. "How do you manage to make everything dirty?"

"It's a gift. But, enough about me. Spill." Ford held his hands up just as I opened my mouth. "Wait! Burke, hand me a beer. I need to get comfy for this bedtime story."

"You're an ass," Burke grumbled but still got a beer out of the fridge and handed it to Ford.

After popping the top, Ford waved a hand at me. "Proceed."

"I'm not telling you about my sex life with Aiden."

"So, you admit you *have* a sex life with Aiden."

I hung my head and laughed. "Yes, Ford, and that's all I'm saying."

"Then what's going on, Cole?" Noah asked as he sat down next to me.

I spent the next hour venting to my friends, getting more and more worked up. They listened, as they always did, and I just poured my heart out. By the end of the convo, I felt better and even more confident that I had done the right thing.

Knowing I was falling was scary enough, but having no clue if I'd land on my feet terrified me. I wanted so much to know if

Aiden was falling, too. If he was, would he land next to me? I wanted him to with every part of my being, but I also needed to know if we were truly in this together. He'd said if he was in a relationship he wanted that person to give their all. Well, he had me. I just had to get up the courage to make that crystal clear.

CHAPTER 16

COLE

"I'm sorry, miss, but unfortunately I can't control the weather." I slapped on a fake smile, which I was getting really good at, if I did say so myself.

"Your brochure shows pictures of sunny beaches. It rained the entire time we were here. That's false advertising!" The woman, seemingly in her mid-twenties, glared at me. Her friends behind her nodded their heads in snide agreement.

"Again, I can't control the weather. A few days ago, we had nothing but sunshine. Unfortunately, Florida is also known for its rain." I glanced at Miss Margie, but quickly looked away when I saw she was seconds away from bursting into laughter. What was I? The god of rain?

"This ruined our whole girls' weekend. This is our last night here, and the weather says rain *again* tomorrow! If you don't want a bad review, you need to do something about this."

What I wanted to say: *Be my fucking guest. I'd love for other people to hear how ridiculous you are.*

What I actually said: "Just give me one second." I tapped a

couple of things into the computer, pulling up their room number then compared it with the restaurant's records. *Bingo.* I exhaled for dramatic effect. *And the award for best actor goes to…* "Okay, it was a longshot, but I can make this happen. What I can do for you *lovely* ladies is make you a reservation in our hotel restaurant for dinner. Unfortunately, it won't include alcohol, but you won't pay a single penny more toward your meals. Oceanside Bar and Grill has amazing cuisine. You won't be disappointed."

Miss Margie turned away, pretending to straighten the back counter—the *immaculate* back counter. Her shoulders shook, and I had to bite my tongue to keep a straight face while the girls huddled in a discussion.

Finally, *Lovely* Leader turned back around with a smug smile. "We figure it's the least you can do."

"Excellent." I went about making the reservation, keeping my face as impassive as I possibly could. "All right, ladies. You are all set for eight in our Oceanside dining room. The meal will include an appetizer for the table, plus dinner and dessert for all four of you. I made sure to reserve you a table by the window with a view of the ocean." *Because it's no extra cost to us.*

"That's more like it," she said smugly. The girls headed for the door, their giggles and whispering echoing in the lobby. One of them said to Lovely Leader, "Trina, you are *sooo* fierce."

Trina replied arrogantly, "I'm the wrong person to mess with. My daddy didn't raise a fool."

Once the door to the lobby closed, with the headache-inducing guests on the other side, Miss Margie lost it. Slapping my arm, she said through hiccups of laughter, "That dinner was included in their package deal!"

"Yup." I grinned proudly.

"They already paid for it!"

"Yup. That's why I never once mentioned I was comping it, but I also didn't lie. They won't pay a penny more than they already have unless, by some miracle, they have some morals and tip the server. If they don't, I'll compensate whoever gets stuck with their table."

Miss Margie and I tried to get ourselves under control. It wasn't often something worked out so perfectly, but that was a win.

"It's nice to see you laughing." Hearing my mother's voice, I whipped my head toward the lobby.

"What are you doing here?" I asked, kicking myself when my mom flinched from my poor delivery. "I mean, you're always *welcome* here."

Her eyes softened. "Can we talk?"

"Yeah." I glanced at Miss Margie. "Let me know if you need me again."

"I sure will, Cole." Miss Margie went around the counter and gave my mother a big hug which was returned just as warmly. "It's so good to see you, Helen. Your son is a bit of a genius, not to mention an amazing boss."

My mom's watery eyes shifted to me. "He's an amazing man, Margie."

I cleared my throat, nudging my head at the hallway. "Why don't we go in my office?"

She followed me back to the small office I shared with Levi. As soon as he saw us, he greeted my mom with a kiss on the cheek and gave us some privacy.

My mom's gaze landed on the bouquet of gorgeous flowers on my desk. "Those are beautiful."

"Aren't they? They're from Aiden. Miss Margie worked her magic over the last few days, so they're still going strong."

"What were they for?"

"To put a smile on my face." What do you know? Said smile spread across my face, thinking of Aiden and how the guy went out of his way to let me know he cared.

I watched my mom's reaction, trying to gauge it as she dropped her eyes. "That was really sweet of him."

"He's a really sweet man." I sat down at my desk, waving a hand at the chair next to it for my mother to sit. "Do you know, in all the time Drake was in my life, he never sent me flowers? None of my ex-boyfriends did. I'm not saying I need all that, but it sure did feel good to know Aiden was thinking about me." I leaned my elbows on my desk, scrubbing my face before clasping my hands together. "Mom, Aiden is someone I never expected to have in my life. This whole thing really caught me by surprise, but it's the best thing that's ever happened to me. Even if Aiden and I don't work out—and I'm going to fight like hell to make sure we do—he's made me see I deserve more than Drake ever gave me. I deserve dates in public. I deserve someone being faithful. I deserve more than being someone's dirty little secret. You keep saying you want me to be happy, but you're not hearing me when I tell you I *am* happy."

"You're absolutely right. Cole, I never meant to hurt you. It's just…you have no idea what it's like to watch your child get hurt over and over again. I thought about what you said, and well, maybe Jim's…maybe we're *all* being too hard on Aiden. If what you're saying is true, and Jim's been the one rejecting Aiden and not the other way around, well…I'm not okay with that. I have one son whom I would die for." I gripped her hand, tears welling up in my eyes. I saw the same emotions reflected back in hers. "I could never imagine turning my back on you, no matter how stubborn we *both* can be." She released a watery laugh, and I handed her a tissue.

I stood up, yanking my mom up into a hug. My cell phone vibrated on my desk, but seeing it was Sage, I let it go to voicemail. "You're stuck with me."

"You're stuck with me, too." She sniffled. I ignored my cell phone ringing again and handed her another tissue. "I truly do mean it this time. I'd like you to bring Aiden over for dinner. Any man who can make you this happy gets my stamp of approval."

"I'll ask—" My desk phone started ringing and I held up one finger. "Sorry, I have to get this one." My heart sped up when I saw Sage's name on the caller ID. "Sage, what's—"

"Why haven't you been answering your damn phone?"

"I'm sorry, I—"

"Aiden needs you." Sage was an emotional person, but it wasn't often he let himself cry. The unmistakable sound in my ear scared the hell out of me.

"What's going on? Where?" Adrenaline pumped through me so rapidly I lost my balance and landed in my chair. The thought of something happening to him…

"Uncle Jim had a heart attack."

This was Aiden's worst fear come to life. "Oh my god. Is he…?"

AIDEN

I felt numb, yet simultaneously every muscle in my entire body ached as I white-knuckled the steering wheel. Sage promised to call Cole because I was afraid I wouldn't be able to get the words out. The frantic beat of my pulse combined with overwhelming fear made it hard enough to concentrate on the road. I knew if I heard Cole's voice, I'd break down immediately. That's what Cole had become to me. My safe place. I needed him so much right now it terrified me almost as much as my desperation to get to the hospital. *What if I'm too late?* "Fuck!" I slammed my hand down on the steering wheel, taking a sharp turn into the hospital parking lot. Pulling into the first spot I saw, I barely shut off the car before jumping out and racing for the Emergency Room entrance.

Billy rushed into my arms, her sobbing scaring the shit out of me. "Billy, talk to me. What happened?"

She brushed tears from her puffy, red eyes, as she sucked in a few quick breaths. "I don't know. One minute he was fine, the next he was having trouble breathing and clutching his chest." She hiccupped and I brushed the hair away from her tear-stained face. "I had some aspirin in my office because, no matter what he said, I wasn't taking any chances. The ambulance showed up not long after, but since I got here, all I've been able to find out is that he's alive."

"Shit." After a few minutes of trying, I wasn't able to get much more info out of the person behind the desk, other than they were trying to stabilize him.

"Aiden!" It was the voice I needed to hear. The second Cole pulled me into his arms, I just broke down, sobbing into his shoulder, gripping the back of his shirt in my tightly fisted hands. "I'm here. I got you." We stayed like that for what felt like hours. He held me up, held all my shattered pieces in place, and I loved him for it.

Jesus Christ, I loved him.

It was never more clear to me than in that moment—as I was faced with the possibility of losing the father I loved—that the man I loved was allowing me to fall apart in his arms. I felt safe letting go because I knew Cole would put me back together. My emotions—heartbreaking fear and overwhelming relief—warred with each other.

Another hand rubbed my back; I wasn't sure whose. I took some deep, trembling breaths, pulling myself together as best as I could. Kissing him softly, I leaned my forehead against his, my voice a hoarse whisper. "Thank you for being here. I really needed you here. I just need you."

"Always. I will always be here for you."

"Have the doctors told you anything?" the gentle female voice from behind me asked, startling me. I assumed it was Billy rubbing my back, but when I turned, I was faced with Cole's mom. She offered me a sympathetic smile, her other arm wrapped around Billy, who was still crying.

Just days before, Cole had stood up to her, for him and for me. I was blown away by how much he was taking charge of his own life. Amazed by the fact he thought I was worth taking a stand for. I never wanted to cause him any trouble with his mom, but the truth was, if it hadn't been me, it would have been someone else. Helen was protective of her son, almost to a fault, yet I envied the way she loved Cole. She had her moments of going overboard, but there was no doubt she would do anything for her son, and she would never turn her back on him.

"No, I haven't heard much other than they're trying to stabilize him."

"Okay, then we'll wait. I know it's hard, but the best thing to do is let them do their jobs." She took my hand in her smaller one and led me over to a chair. I clung to Cole with my other hand, pulling him down into the seat next to me.

"I'm sorry! I got here as soon as I could. I had to call in extra help to cover the restaurant." Sage jogged through the waiting room and right into Billy's arms, his eyes flicking to Helen in confusion before locking back on mine. "Any news?" he asked, sitting down in the chair beside Cole while pulling his sister into the seat next to him.

I shook my head, allowed Billy to relay the story, all the while clinging to Cole's hand, my other one, oddly enough, still in Helen's.

We sat in silence. Memories of my childhood flipped through my mind like an old reel. My pop had always been my hero. I'd looked up to him, had wanted to be like him, had followed him around the small craft brewery every day. Somewhere along the way, that had changed. Somewhere along the way, I had trouble blending the man who'd always been my hero with the man who, as I got older, had fought tooth and nail against every suggestion I made toward the business. I had difficulty understanding why a man I had always looked up to, didn't trust my opinions or take me seriously. Maybe it hadn't been my place, though, to question why Rafferty's hadn't changed since it opened its doors. And, because I hadn't accepted the family business for what it was…

"This is my fault." The words came out before I could think twice about them.

"What? No, it's not." Cole's hand tightened around mine. I looked up at him, seeing both Billy and Sage giving me confused looks on the other side of him.

"It is. I should have taken over Rafferty's years ago. If I had, maybe he would have retired." I lowered my head. "Maybe he wouldn't be here right now."

"Don't even think it, Aiden," Billy snapped, tearing up again. "You know I've been offering to take over that place for years. I love Rafferty's. Hell, Scott was even ready to quit his job and run the place with me. I bet Uncle Jim never told you that part, though. I may not have the Rafferty last name anymore, but I'm still a Rafferty."

I shot to my feet and pulled her into my arms. "I'm sorry, of course you are. I didn't mean you couldn't handle it. You're the only reason that place is still up and running."

"I know what you meant." Billy pulled back and took my face in her hands. "I think we're all a little on edge, but you didn't do anything wrong, Aiden. SandBar is something to be proud of. If Rafferty's were mine…well, I guess it doesn't matter, does it? Uncle Jim is going to be fine and back to being his stubborn, bossy self in no time."

I kissed her on the top of her raven hair. "Yeah, he will," I agreed, trying like hell to believe it.

I took my seat again next to Cole, immediately taking his

hand. It felt like hours before someone finally came to update us. "Aiden Rafferty?"

"That's me." I jumped up from my chair, meeting the doctor halfway. "Is he okay?" My voice cracked, but there Cole was, right by my side again, holding my hand, giving me strength.

"I'm Doctor Wilson. Your father suffered a mild heart attack. We were able to stabilize him, and the response he had to the medications indicates there was no serious damage to his heart. We'll need to monitor him, run some tests to be sure, but as long as the results are okay, he'll be able to go home in a day or two."

All I heard out of that whole thing was *heart attack*. Two words I'd been dreading ever since he started having his so-called heartburn. "Can I see him?"

"For a few minutes."

"Can I bring my partner?" I pulled Cole closer, heard a gasp of surprise leave him before he held tighter to my hand.

The doctor gave a warm smile to Cole before looking back at me. "Of course. He'll be groggy and needs his rest, but the two of you can go back and see him." The doctor looked around me to Billy, Sage, and Cole's mom. "It might be best if the rest of you come back tomorrow during visiting hours."

"Yes, I'm sure Jim needs his rest," Cole's mom responded. As the doctor walked away, Helen turned to me. "You let me know if you need anything. Anything at all. I'm going to stop at the store on my way home. Jim will need some healthy, mild food in his house. I remember when my own father had a heart attack he was on a special diet for a while."

"Thank you, Helen."

She kissed my cheek then wrapped her arms around me. I hadn't felt a mother's hug in over a decade, but I was grateful for it now. She placed a hand on Cole's cheek. "I see it now," she whispered. "You stay with Aiden. I'll take the car. I've got everything else under control."

Cole wrapped his mom in a hug, his breath shuddering against her shoulder. “Thanks, Mom.” As she walked to the exit with Billy and Sage, Cole turned to me. “You’ve done it now. You’ve unleashed Mama Sullivan. Prepare yourself for more food than you’ll ever be able to eat and coddling to the highest degree.”

“I can handle that.” I held Cole’s hand as a nurse led us to my pop. My breath caught at the sight of him. He was ghostly pale and looked so fragile, I was afraid to get too close. His eyes were closed, but my gaze fell to the only thing that mattered in that moment…the rise and fall of his chest. We’d get through the rest of it later. Things had to change, there was no question about that, but first he had to heal.

“Pop,” I said softly, keeping my voice low so as not to disturb him. I took his hand gently. “I’m here, and I love you. You scared the hell outta me.” I sucked in a shaky breath and let the tears fall. I didn’t care if he could hear the emotion in my voice. I’d almost lost him today. I felt the slightest movement against my fingers, the ever-so-gentle pressure of him letting me know he heard me. He opened his eyes briefly, but his eyelids seemed too heavy for him and he slid them closed again. “I’ll be back tomorrow,” I whispered quickly before he drifted off too deeply to hear me.

Cole drove my car home, my body limp against the passenger-side door. Jesse had assured me, when I’d gotten the call about my pop, that she had the bar taken care of. She was my second-in-command at SandBar, and I trusted her implicitly. I called her on the way home and updated her on his condition. I didn’t care what he said, when he got home, I was taking care of him for as long as the doctor suggested. That meant I’d be at the bar less, but Jesse immediately stepped up, reassuring me she had it all under control. With Pop under the care of doctors and nurses in the hospital, and SandBar in Jesse’s capable hands, I gave myself permission to just *be*. Be afraid, be sad, be emotionally exhausted.

Cole didn’t waste any time opening my car door, taking my

hand to help me out, and using my keys to unlock my front door. Locking us both inside the house, Cole led me to my bedroom, his soft fingers brushing over my skin as he undressed me down to my underwear. After maneuvering me into bed, he took a step toward the door and I quickly grabbed his hand.

"Where are you going?" Even I couldn't deny the panic in my voice. When had I come to need him so desperately?

"I'll be right back. I'm just getting you some water." He smiled softly down at me, squeezing my hand gently before letting me go.

He was back in less than a minute, setting two water glasses down on the nightstand. Cole removed all his clothes except his black briefs and slid under the sheet, cuddling up to my side, his head on my shoulder. He felt like the only tangible thing I could hold to keep me grounded. We lay there in silence for…I didn't even know how long. All I knew was the overwhelming panic that had grabbed ahold of me a few hours ago was finally starting to release its painful grasp. Cole ran his finger through the thin layer of hair on my chest; the path, one he followed whenever we were together like this, always lulled me into a deep calmness.

Whether it was from exhaustion or feeling safe in his arms, I closed my eyes and drifted off to sleep.

CHAPTER 17

AIDEN

When I woke up, Cole's warm body wrapped around me, I was so tempted to roll him beneath me and taste every inch of him. My hand lazily ran up and down his back, his steady breathing in tune with each pass over his skin. I felt a soft kiss to the side of my chest and glanced down, seeing Cole's gorgeous blue eyes as he peered up at me. I could tell by the way his fingers found that path again on my chest, how his eyes darkened and he bit his bottom lip…he was offering me comfort, a chance to forget, but…

"Overthinking isn't something you do, remember?" Cole said. "Your dad, your loyalty, your need to let me know this is more than just sex. I know it is." He pushed up on his forearm and leaned over me. "There is no one else in this bed but you and me, so can we stop letting past mistakes get in our way? Respecting me is one thing, but holy shit do I need to feel you inside me." He slid his hand down my chest, cupping my cock, the thin material of my boxer briefs doing nothing to stop how quickly my cock was filling—not that I'd stop it, even if I could. "I won't let anyone else ruin what we have, but I won't pressure you either. Just know I'm ready when—*mmpf…*"

I silenced Cole with my lips, pushing him back onto the mattress, taking control as I pushed my tongue into his mouth. I didn't need to hear any more. I *did* respect him. That included trusting when he said he was ready because, fuck, I wanted him. Feeling him underneath me, his long legs spreading in invitation, his eager hips pushing up, rubbing our covered cocks together—he was as desperate for me as I was for him.

I broke the kiss long enough to push his briefs down and off his legs, removing mine and tossing them both to the floor. When I settled back between his thighs, our leaking dicks lining up, I buried my face in his neck and just took a minute to *feel.* The coarse hair on his calves brushing mine, the strength of his thighs from running, his balls pressed against me where my groin met my hip. He felt so fucking right in my arms—all man and all mine. There wasn't a part of me that didn't want him, to be as close to him as humanly possible.

Traveling down the side of his neck, I licked a path to the hollow above his collarbone, loving how his hands slid into the back of my hair and held on. The fact that he could believe, even for a moment, that there was anything lacking about him blew my mind. The emotional connection I felt with him surpassed any I'd ever had, and I hadn't even buried myself inside him yet. I lived for every moan, every sting of my hair being pulled, or hoarse groan he let out when I did something he liked.

I'd tasted every inch of him over the last month, except for my current destination. I was going to stop and partake in every little nook and cranny along the way there. I teased his nipple into a peak, grazing my teeth over the brown disc. Hard muscle under smooth, tanned skin covering his chest—I was obsessed with feeling his strength. Tracing the valleys defining his abs with my tongue, my chin brushed the wet tip of his cock as I dipped my tongue into his bellybutton.

"Aiden.." he rasped out. "Please…"

"I'm here. I got you." As the words passed my lips, I recognized them as the same ones he'd said to me at the hospital earlier. I wanted to say so much more, but hearing Cole suck in quick, short breaths, seeing his eyes screwed shut, head pushed back on the pillow…he was already floating too high to hear them. The place he was in, though, was so fucking sexy I lost all thought other than to make him lose his mind—to make him mine.

Cole whimpered, rocking his hips, making it clear what he wanted. He hadn't held back his desires in weeks. It was my turn to show him how much I needed him. Use my hands, my mouth, my tongue, my cock every-fucking-where on his body until he was trembling and shouting out my name.

But first…

Cole moaned, "Yes, finally," when I slid my mouth down over his cock. I laughed through my nose, smiling around his dick in my mouth. Jesus, sex with him—anything with him—was fun… exhilarating…*right.* Cole looked down the length of his lean body at me, traced my taut lips as they stretched around his cock. "So fucking sexy like this."

I breathed in through my nose, my eyes sliding closed. Fun was great, but when he looked at me like that, whispered words like that to me, it was the hottest fucking thing. I worked his cock, gliding my tongue over the soft skin covering his erection, sucking on my way to the tip, teasing that spot right under his head that he loved. *I could do this all night.*

That wasn't the end goal, though, and I sure as hell wanted that trophy. I gripped both of his thighs and pushed them up toward his chest. Letting his wet cock slide from my mouth, I kissed down its glistening length. Instead of sucking one of his balls into my mouth, I pushed his legs back even farther. The second I blew hot air onto Cole's hole, his eyes popped open, eyebrows raised to his hairline as he watched me. And because he was so enthralled, I locked eyes with him, stuck my tongue out, and circled it around his puckered entrance.

"Oh *fuck*… Oh my god, Aiden…" His head sprang up and down on a trampoline made of cotton, caught between looking at me while I ate his ass and cursing out in pleasure as his head bounced back onto the pillow. "You—*holy shit*…"

I didn't answer with words, just continued my feast and reached my hand out. He didn't need words to figure out what I wanted, anyway. Cole reached over to the nightstand, grabbing the bottle of lube and shoving it into my hand. I seized the perfect moment—when he was distracted, fishing around blindly for a condom in my drawer—to breach him with just the tip of my tongue. Cole's reaction was priceless. His back arched as he cried out, yanking back on his own thighs, completely offering himself to me. So. Fucking. Sexy.

"Your finger, your tongue, your dick… I don't care. For the love of… Just do it!" He tossed the condom at me, the foil packet bouncing off my head and hitting the mattress.

Another chuckle left my lips, my warm breath grazing his hole. Sitting back on my haunches, I clicked the bottle open, squeezing a good amount to coat my fingers. "I fucking love"—I ran my middle finger around his opening—"when you tell me"—I pushed the tip into his silky heat—"what you want. I'll do anything you tell me to right now. That's how fucking hot it is."

"Then get that damn finger inside me and get the job done, Aiden…and two of his buddies. Pinky and thumb need not apply."

I barked out a laugh, the sound morphing into a groan to finally have some part of me inside him. His body loosened for me, taking all three fingers in a matter of minutes. My lube-covered hands shook as I tried to open the condom. To say I was desperate to be inside him was an understatement.

Cole pushed up into a sitting position, his legs still on either side of me. "Give it here," he whispered, pecking me on the lips. He didn't open the packet, though. Instead, he swung around onto his knees, leaning over until his mouth was in front of my cock. On a sigh, he grabbed hold of my shaft and sank his mouth down over it.

My head fell back in pure fucking ecstasy. "Shit, Cole…" Small whimpers hummed from his throat, vibrating against my throbbing cock, sending shockwaves straight to my toes. Cole slid his mouth all the way down, taking me to the back of his throat. When he breathed me in through his nose, I gripped the sheets on either side of me, trying to stave off my orgasm.

Then he fucking swallowed, and the hot tunnel of his throat constricted around my shaft. Eyes crossing, fists tightening, nails digging into the sheets, I bit my bottom lip hard, calling on every ounce of willpower I had so as not to shoot off right then and there. "Feels so good. Fuck, Cole…if you don't stop I'm gonna come."

My dick popped out of his mouth and he sat up, wiping off his chin. "Not that I wouldn't enjoy sucking the come right out of you, but tonight I need to feel you come deep inside me."

"The things you say to me." The thought of going bare, truly coming inside him, holy shit that made me crazy, but that's what Cole did to me. He made me desperately want everything with him.

Cole removed the condom from the wrapper then slowly rolled it down my painfully hard erection. Kissing me again, I got lost in those lips until he pulled away, coated his hand in lube, and lay back down. My eyes zeroed in on his fist sliding up and down his hard cock. "It's still crazy to me to see you look at me like that."

I raised my gaze. "Like what?" Cole shook his head, biting his bottom lip, so I asked again, "Looking at you like what?"

He paused for a couple more seconds, but something changed in his eyes when he whispered, "The way that I look at you." It was a completely raw, genuinely shocked, incredibly brave admission for someone who'd been hurt before.

"Jesus, baby." I'd never called him that. Apparently, tonight was a night of firsts. Unsure if the surprise on his face was good or bad, I leaned down, holding myself over him, and crashed my mouth to his.

He pulled his legs back up to his chest, his thighs boxing me in. I shimmied closer, lining my cock up with his hole, but holy shit, I was not prepared for the sheer magnitude of pleasure that shot through me from his body tightening like a vice around my cock. Forcing myself to pause, I waited for him to give me the green light to go farther. Cole's feet landed on my ass, pulling me toward him. Just the signal I was looking for.

My arms locked, holding me above him, as I drove into him in measured thrusts. I didn't want to hurt him, paying close attention to his reactions while chasing the raging need to bury myself in him.

"Harder, baby," Cole pleaded, yanking my face down to kiss me, his tongue plowing into my mouth while my cock plowed into his ass. I could feel his hand pumping his cock between us. I wanted to push it away, to own every part of his orgasm, but my sanity was on the brink, my head foggy from the need to come. *I'll be damned if I lose it first.*

Forcing my lips away from his, I pushed up to a kneeling position, grabbed hold of his thighs, and pounded into him. Sweat dripped down my temples, my chest, but his cries of *More!* and *Right there!* fueled me to keep pushing. I tagged that bundle of nerves inside him over and over again, feeling like a fucking king every time he shouted my name or arched his back in bone-deep pleasure.

Cole's hand flew over his cock in rapid strokes, his muscles bunching up tight, his neck straining. "Oh fuck!" He pushed his head back into the pillow as white hot liquid shot out of his dick, landing on his stomach, his body twitching with release. It was only then I allowed myself to let go.

I fell forward and I wrapped my arms around him, holding him as close to me as I could, my hips thrusting, my face buried in his neck as my orgasm tore through me. It felt like my body spasmed forever, yet it was over too soon.

Trembling, I pulled back enough to see his face, sucking in a breath at how thoroughly debauched he looked—happily floating on that cloud of post-orgasm bliss, his hair matted to his face with sweat, the skin around his mouth red from my stubble. He was so damn gorgeous, and when he gave me a half-lidded smile and kissed me softly, I came undone. For the second time that day, I knew it didn't matter, because Cole was the glue that held me together.

CHAPTER 18

COLE

"Cole, how's Jim doing?" Noah asked, the smell of pizza filling my house. The guys all stopped what they were doing and waited for me to answer.

"He's getting there. We think he's coming home sometime tomorrow. I was with Aiden at the hospital earlier, but he wanted to check in on the bar then go back and sit with his dad a bit. He's there now."

"He must have been so scared." Noah smiled sadly. He knew all too well the pain of losing a parent. "He's lucky to have you."

"Pretty sure I'm the lucky one." I was definitely the lucky one. I still couldn't believe how much my life had changed in just a couple of months. It was hard to believe that not long before Memorial Day, I struggled to see my life without Drake, to the point that I let him use me, and now I had a man like Aiden in my life. He blew me away every single day showing me how much he cared about me. With him, I never wondered if I was enough.

"Oh man. I'm gonna get sick of seeing that cheesy, lovesick face real quick if you don't knock it the hell off." Burke dropped down on my couch, a plate with two loaded, extra cheese—as they should be—slices of pizza in his hand.

Noah slapped the side of Burke's thigh with the back of his hand. "Leave him alone. I think it's amazing. About damn time he found someone who knows his worth."

"Yeah, yeah. He's happy…butterflies and unicorns and puppies *happy*, and Aiden isn't a dick. We get it." Burke threw his arm up, blocking the pillow I tossed at him. "Hey, if I drop this greasy shit on your carpet, it won't be my fault."

"Don't be jealous just because my man is fucking hot." *My man.* Damn, that felt good to say. This newfound confidence, in myself and in what I had with Aiden, was so foreign, but I wouldn't trade it for anything.

Burke opened his mouth to argue, but exhaled instead, puffing out his cheeks. "Damn it, I can't even deny that one."

No, he couldn't. I sank back in my chair with a smug smile, basking in the glory that, for once, I had a man who truly cared about me—who also happened to fuck me better than anyone ever had, and who also happened to be sexy as hell.

"What are you doing over there?" Levi asked, brows furrowed as he studied Ford.

Ford didn't answer, so I nudged his foot with mine.

"What?" He looked around. "What'd I miss?"

"Uh, pretty much everything since you've been glued to your phone all night." Levi set his plate down on the coffee table and leaned back against the couch. I'd really started to pay attention to the signs we'd all been missing for who knew how long now. Problem was, those signals were only coming from one of my friends, not the other.

"Sorry. I, uh…I got a friend suggestion on Facebook the other day. Guy I went to high school with. So, I sent him a friend request, and it took him fucking forever to accept it." Ford frowned at his screen, thumbing up the glass as he scrolled through pictures.

"Were you"—Levi cleared his throat—"with that guy?" His eyes flicked to me then quickly shifted away, his cheeks getting pink.

Ford drew up his mouth in a part sex-on-the-brain/part cocky-bastard smirk. "Horizontally? Yes. And vertically, and behind—"

Levi's hand shot up. "We get the picture."

"Gave the guy my V-card." Ford shrugged one shoulder like it was no big deal, but clearly, it had meant something. Why else would he be stalking this guy's page? "He was cute as hell back then, in a geeky sorta way. What is it about smart guys that's so fucking hot? Don't get me wrong, I held my own, but this guy was valedictorian of our class. Went to Harvard. I lost track of him after that. I'll tell you one thing, though. The guy ain't so cute anymore."

Relief flooded Levi's face as Ford continued to scroll through the photos. That was until Ford stopped on one and turned the phone so we all could see the man he'd been obsessing over for the last hour. "He's fucking *hot*. Like, drinking the sexy juice, yoga bendy, lips you wanna snack on—and I *did*—hot."

"Yoga bendy?" I snorted.

Ford flipped to one more picture of the guy doing some kind of shirtless yoga pose, his lean muscles tensed and defined. "Yoga bendy." He flipped through a few more with narrowed eyes. "And, apparently, not single. He hasn't posted anything in a while, so I guess I forgive him for taking so damn long." It didn't stop him from staring at his phone for the rest of the night, getting awkward glances from Levi.

When they all got up and cleaned up their mess, I grabbed Levi's arm. This was possibly a monumentally bad idea, but… "Can I talk to you?"

He gave me a strange look but nodded. "Yeah, sure."

Burke, Ford, and Noah were as loud as usual, filing out my front door. It wasn't until the door closed that I realized how clammy my hands were. *Maybe this isn't such a—*

"So, what's up? Everything okay?" Levi leaned back against the counter, his arms crossed over his chest. He was a gorgeous man, all pouty lips and soul-deep eyes. None of us had ever crossed that line, though. Our friendship was too important, or at least, that was what we'd always said.

"Actually, I just wanted to make sure everything is okay with you."

Levi's back straightened, his eyes landing everywhere but on mine. "Yeah. Why wouldn't it be?"

Okay, so…not going as planned… "You just seem off. I don't know." Brilliant execution—you know, in the *off with his head* sort of way, considering I was accomplishing nothing with my skilled line of questioning. *Where's Noah when I need him? Oh, right…he just left because you thought this was something you could do on your own.* Instead of digging myself in deeper, I said, "I'm here. If you ever need to talk. Doesn't matter about what… or who."

Levi swallowed hard but nodded. When he got to the front door and opened it, I panicked, not wanting to miss the opportunity to say something. I grabbed his arm, stopping him before he walked out.

"Look, I know more than most about unrequited love. You know that." I thought back to the night Aiden changed everything, and oddly enough, it wasn't the one where he'd claimed to be my boyfriend. "Sometimes…sometimes we're so focused on one thing, one *person*, that we can't see past them. Thing is, while you're focused on that one person, someone else is waving their arms in the air, doing everything they can in hopes you'll finally see them." *Or the light they're extending to guide you out of that black tunnel.* Aiden didn't just offer me that light. He *was* my light in the darkness. I knew that wholeheartedly now.

"Aiden made me realize two things throughout all this. One, unrequited love isn't always real love. Sometimes that person is really an asshole…or you love someone but confuse that with being *in* love. Two, maybe who you're meant to be with is actually standing right in front of you, but it's not the person you think. Maybe it's worth a try to look past that unrequited love to see if you can find something real."

I dropped his arm and exhaled. "Jeez, I'm rambling. It all made sense in my head."

Levi pulled me into a hug and I wrapped my arms around him. "Thank you. I promise I'm okay, but…" He pulled back, his sad eyes crushing me under their weight. I knew what he was feeling all too well. "I'm not sure it's that easy. I get what you mean, though. I'll give it some thought, okay?"

"Everything alright?" That deep timbre was a sound I could happily hear for the rest of my life. Aiden stood on the walkway looking back and forth between me and Levi. "I can come back… walk around the block…"

"No, it's fine," Levi rushed out. "I was just leaving." He kissed my temple before walking past Aiden, shaking his hand on the way by. "He's all yours."

Aiden's mouth tipped up on one side. "Damn right. All mine.""

I met him halfway, wrapping my arms around his neck. I could feel how tired he was as he sighed against my shoulder. "How's he doing?"

"The same. Mostly sleeping when I was there." He held me so incredibly tight. I wanted to always be that comfort for him. His light in the dark.

His hair was still wet from the shower, damp against my

fingers. "You know, you can take a shower here. You don't have to go home first."

"I needed to get the smell of hospital off me, and I knew as soon as I walked in this door, I wouldn't be able to keep my hands off you."

"Well, when you put it that way…"

He pulled me inside the house, closing in on me until my back bounced against the wall inside the foyer, then he kicked the door closed behind him. He swooped in, stealing the breath from my lungs as he plunged his tongue in my mouth. I would never get tired of this. Even just kissing him made every nerve ending come alive.

Pressing my palm against Aiden's chest, I moved him back. He willingly let me guide his backward steps into the living room. "It's a shame these clean clothes are about to land on my living room floor."

"Clean is overrated. Messy is so much more fun." Aiden tore his shirt over his head and tossed it aside.

"You know, I realized something today," I said, unbuttoning his jeans and shoving my hand down the front.

"What's that?" he groaned, pushing his cock against my hand.

I peeled back the waistband of his underwear, swiping my finger across the tip of his cock, gathering his pre-come. Slowly, I slid my finger into my mouth, coating my tongue with his flavor, my eyes drifting closed.

"Jesus," he hissed.

I opened my eyes again, ghosting my lips against his, my tongue darting out, licking his bottom lip. "I haven't tasted you yet."

Aiden pulled back to look at me. "You just did." Holding his gaze, I slid my hand into his boxer briefs and around to his ass, running my finger up the seam. "*Oh…*"

"That something you'd be into?" I dipped my finger into the valley of his ass, watching his reaction as I traced his hole.

Aiden's eyes fell closed, his head rolling back. "Fuck, yes." He swallowed hard and licked his lips, his body jerking when I pressed my finger against his opening. With my free hand, I cradled the back of his head, making him look at me. I fucking soared on the power he gave me, the way he let me take what I wanted, the strength coursing through my veins because I had the ability to make him fall apart.

I leaned in, pulling my hand from his pants, pressing my lips against his ear. "Everything off." He met my eyes as he took a step back, held my gaze while he pushed his jeans and underwear down. He kicked off his sneakers, removing every stitch of clothing. Waiting for my next move, he stood there naked in my living room, his hard cock jutting out in front of him, the tip leaking. He was fucking loving this.

I thought about taking my clothes off, but there was something powerful in the way he stood before me completely naked, surrendering to me while I was fully clothed. As if he was saying he was mine to do with whatever I wanted—and fuck, did I want things. Messy fucking things.

Wrapping my hand around his cock, I guided him over to the couch. "Fuck," he hissed, apparently turned on by my use of his dick as a way to make him follow me. I stood him in front of the curtained window. No one could actually see in, but the idea that his naked silhouette could possibly be seen was hot as fuck. Aiden looked back over his shoulder at the window then met my eyes with an overwhelming intensity. I held my breath, waiting for any kind of sign he wasn't into this.

Instead, he turned to the side, his cock proudly protruding. I imagined the silhouette of his profile from the other side of that window. What he would look like. Funny how my views on the subject had completely changed. I didn't really want anyone to see us, but I was totally turned on by the possibility that they could anyway. That as I got on my knees and took Aiden's cock into my mouth, someone could be watching. It was the fact that I no longer worried that the thing I loved most—sucking a big cock, feeling its girth as my throat closed around it—was the only thing I knew how to do well. Damn right I did it well, and I wasn't ashamed of that. I was confident I knew how to make Aiden's eyes roll back in his head.

And I was about to prove that even more right now.

I dropped to my knees and sucked him to the back of my throat, moaning around his cock. His hands clenched clumps of my hair to the point of pain, the sting so fucking good. I pulled out the packets I'd stuck in my pocket earlier, dropping them on the couch. Feeling his legs tremble, I gave up on the window fantasy, maneuvering him to the couch. Releasing his cock from my mouth, I pushed him down onto the cushions, knee-walking until my thighs were flush with the couch, my body between Aiden's legs. Jesus, I was ravenous to taste him and quickly shoved his thighs back, my mouth covering his hole, my tongue finding the meal I'd been craving.

"Oh fuck, Cole." Aiden cupped the back of my head, holding me there like I had any intention of leaving. Hell no. I was nowhere near done with him. Pointing my tongue, I slipped the tip inside him, over and over again. I feasted like it was my last fucking meal, needing more. I began at his hole and worked my way to the tip of his cock, sucking each ball into my mouth, licking the vein that ran up his shaft, tonguing his slit, his pre-come making my mouth water. I'd never heard Aiden make those sounds before and damn did it drive me crazy that I was responsible. "Cole…*fuck*…I need…"

He couldn't get the words out, so I took a chance, ripping open the packet I needed while still going to town on his cock. I coated my fingers in lube, pretty sure this was what he was asking for as he rocked his ass against my mouth. I licked a path up his taint, over his balls and the length of his shaft, sucking him into my mouth, my middle finger circling his hole. Victory was mine when I pushed the tip of my finger inside him and he shouted, “Fuck, yes!”

He said he liked it when I was vocal? Jesus Christ, I almost came in my fucking jeans. I worked him slowly, opening his body, feeling his muscles loosen with each added finger. Sucking his cock all the way in again, I buried my nose in his groin while crooking my fingers up, rubbing over his prostate. His grip in my hair tightened, and I fully expected him to come down my throat. But when he groaned out, “Fuck me…Cole. I want you to fuck me,” my eyes popped open, his dick slid out of my mouth, and I stared at him in awe, my jaw dropping.

“Are you serious?” Kind of a weird question to ask when my fingers were still in his ass, but I needed to be really sure I’d heard him right.

“Fuck yeah, I am. Do it.”

Well, folks, I could now proudly say that I held the Guinness World Record for getting naked. No need to check; that title was mine. I wasn’t even sure where half my clothes ended up. The only thing that mattered was the condom I rolled down my aching cock and the look in Aiden’s eyes as I stretched him again with my fingers.

Feeling like his body was ready, I rubbed my mushroom head over his hole. I went slow, watching his reactions, feeling his hand grip my hip tightly when he needed a second to adjust, his fingers eagerly pulling me closer when he wanted more. My hands trembled, one guiding my dick into him, while the other held his thick thigh. When I was gloriously buried inside him, I drew in a huge breath, not even aware I’d been holding it.

“Move, Cole,” Aiden rasped. He moved his hips, gasping in pleasure. “Oh god.”

What was that saying about genies and wishes and commands? Who fucking knew. My brain was scrambled, my body shaking as I pulled my hips back slowly then thrust back in. I didn't have to wonder if it was too hard. Aiden's moaned, "Holy *fuck*, yesss…" was good enough for me.

Drawing my hips back again, I found a steady rhythm—which within minutes was more frantic than anything else. Chasing Aiden's every moan, pegging his prostate the way I knew made me lose my mind, feeling his tight heat wrapped around my cock…it was all too much and not enough. The room filled with the deliciously dirty sounds of my balls hitting his ass, obscene grunting I had absolutely no control over, and the couch hitting the windowsill over and over again.

Aiden was lost in pleasure, the veins in his neck bulging, his skin flushed red, his eyes shut tight. I fisted his cock, pumping it to the beat of every thrust I drove into him. Thank fuck, Aiden opened his eyes and held my stare right before he shouted, his cock unloading, shooting ribbons of come onto my hand and his sweaty stomach. Finally, I was able to let go, and man, did I ever. My body jerked, spasming through every pulse into the condom, every time his body clenched around my shaft, every aftershock that shuddered through him.

I pried my eyes open, the biggest fucking grin spreading across my face as I looked down at him. "Holy shit."

"Holy. Fucking. Shit." Aiden laughed, wincing as I pulled out of him. The second the condom was tied off and tossed onto the floor, Aiden yanked me down, crashing my mouth to his. When we came up for air, he drawled, "Messy is so much more fun."

I barked out a laugh, kissing him again. Truth was, when I was with him, everything was just *more*.

CHAPTER 19

AIDEN

"How am I supposed to live off this tinted water? You call this food?" Pop groused, scrunching his nose at the bowl of soup in front of him.

I held in my laugh, just happy he was back to being his normal ornery self. "Don't let Helen hear you. She cooked that herself, and it isn't bland. I tried it. You're just used to adding salt to your food before you even taste it. Besides, it has a ton of vegetables and grains in it, which you know the doctor said you needed."

He'd spent two days in the hospital and had been home for two, but he was on bed rest for at least the next several days. A fact he was not the least bit happy about. Too bad Billy, Sage, and I didn't care. He was taking a goddamn break whether he wanted to or not. His body had made it perfectly clear he needed one.

"That woman—"

"That woman has been here every day, helping me cook for you and clean up after you and keeping the Walkie Talkies at bay, so you better watch what you say. You know Edna Lawry has her beady little eyes on you. Say the word, and *she* can nurse your cranky ass back to health."

His eyes went comically wide. "You wouldn't dare…" I cocked a challenging eyebrow and smirked. Bristling, he actually looked somewhat shamefaced as he took a bite of the soup. "Well, I guess it's not *that* bad."

"Good call," I said, rolling my eyes at his backhanded compliment.

Inhaling deeply, I geared up for a battle I wasn't sure I was ready for. If there were any signs that he was getting too worked up, the conversation would end immediately, but I had to give it a chance. I knew he was more scared than he was letting on. It felt like a low blow, but it seemed the only way to get him to listen was when that fear was fresh in his mind—and the only way to get the fucking balls to bring it up was when it was fresh in my mine.

"Pop, we need to talk," I began, sitting down in the chair beside his bed to prepare myself for the immediate rejection that always followed. Instead, he looked out his bedroom window, his eerie silence making me on edge.

Finally, he sighed. "I suppose I know what you're gonna say."

Unexpected. "Something's gotta change. I know you're disappointed in me, in the man I've become, but I don't regret starting SandBar. I tried for years to be someone you trusted enough with Rafferty's while still trying to incorporate some of my ideas. It was a losing battle, and quite honestly, with Mom gone, it wasn't one I was willing to fight anymore."

I blinked back tears and wiped my clammy hands on my shorts while he continued looking out the window. Despite feeling like I was talking to myself, I pushed on. "When I came back, I was sure you'd give me that chance because you were right." He finally set unreadable eyes on me. "I wasn't ready to take on a job of that size before I left. I didn't know what the hell I was doing.

So, I took some business courses and worked my way up in a bar in the city. Learned the ins and outs. Hell, I'd even saved enough money to make the upgrades for Rafferty's so I could be an equal part of the business. I believed in it that much, and"—a humorless laugh slipped out—"I truly thought you'd be proud of me. So, where did I go wrong? When did my dreams become ridiculous to you?" *Goddamn voice with its stupid tremble.* I'd been on an emotional rollercoaster for days.

"Bah," he grumbled, waving a hand at me. "I never said your dreams are ridiculous."

"Not out loud."

He exhaled long and slow, scratching the white stubble on his chin as he glanced back out the window. If he was going to finally talk to me about this, I didn't care if he looked at me or not while doing it.

"Losing your mama felt like losing control. I couldn't stop what was happening to her. You took the brunt of that, I guess. Going back to work after losing her and seeing all the changes you'd come up with on paper…well, I guess I couldn't handle it. I'd just had to let go of the reins and leave your mama's fate in God's hands. I wasn't ready to give up control of anything else." He pinned me with a guilty look. "Even to you."

That was the most honest thing he'd said to me in eleven years. I was almost afraid to breathe and ruin the moment. Almost… "What about when I came back?"

Shrugging his shoulders, he lifted the tray with the soup bowl off his lap and toward me. Quickly, I took it, setting it on the dresser by the door before sitting back down.

"Pride, I suppose," he continued. "It's not easy admitting when it's time to throw in the towel." He sighed. "Because you were right, too. Don't give me that look," he griped as I stared at him in shock. "My brother never wanted Rafferty's. He'd made that clear early on. I knew you did, but I'm stubborn. I didn't think you'd actually go out on your own, but ya sure proved me wrong."

"Pop..."

He held up his hand. "Ya did good, son." There was no stopping my shock that time, even if I tried. "SandBar, what you've built there, it's impressive, but it's also clear I've lost the chance to ever have you take over Rafferty's."

The comment hit a nerve, but he was right. There was no way I could run two successful businesses on my own. "Pop, if you don't give Billy that chance, you're a fool. Can't you see how much she loves it? She's ready and you know it. With her running it, Rafferty's *will* stay in the family. I'd even be willing to talk about joining forces. It'll take some time to legally change the name of the bar, not to mention the cost of rebranding."

He blinked several times, his mouth falling open in shock. "You mean you'd change your bar to Rafferty's?"

I laughed, and damn, it felt good. "Let's not get crazy. I'd be okay with...I don't know...something that blends the two places together, *if* it's okay with Billy. This is her decision too because I'm assuming you're gonna swallow your pride and let her take over?" I challenged.

He scowled—he wouldn't be my father if he didn't—but for the first time I knew he was listening to me and taking me seriously. "Go on."

So, I did. "That means changing all the branding on *your* products, too, and offering my craft beer alongside yours. We'd keep the names, but the labels would have to match. We'd also have to change the name above your door to go with whatever we choose for the bar. We could offer deals, drawing business to both places. Ten percent off a flight in our tasting room with purchase of a dinner in the restaurant. Or vice versa."

"Sounds like you've given this some thought, even after everything."

"Yeah, I have." I dropped my gaze to my lap, embarrassed by the emotion cracking my voice. "All I've ever wanted was to make you proud."

"Bah"—he swiped his hand in the air again—"'course I'm proud of you. Maybe even a little jealous, if I'm being honest."

There was one more thing we needed to get out in the open before I let that shock of an admission sink in. "Even if I'm dating Cole Sullivan? You still gonna be proud of me if I'm with a man? Because he's it for me." I hadn't really spoken the words to Cole yet, but I hoped he got the message based on my actions—oh, and the incredible sex. *Not the time to be thinking about that, Aiden.*

"'Course. Why would I have a problem with that? Gay nephew, remember? Besides the fact that my sister-in-law would feed me to the sharks if I did have a problem with it, there ain't nothin' wrong with Sage, and I'd challenge anyone to dare say otherwise."

He had me there. "So, why the dirty look the other day when Cole was holding my hand?"

"Because I'm always the last damn one to find out. Remember how fast you got married to Sasha? I barely knew the girl's name before you were sayin' *I do*."

Well, shit... "You're right. I'm sorry about that. Looks like we both need to work on some things, huh?"

"Yeah, well, almost dying changes a man, ya know?" He rubbed the back of his neck. "The fact that I came close..." He shook his head. "I've been so damn stubborn. If your mama were here, she'd have set me straight a long time ago, but that's where I went wrong. Shouldn't take someone else smoothing things over with my own damn son. I'm sorry about that. I'm sorry I almost left you to beat yourself up for the rest of your life thinking you let me down."

I nodded and grabbed his hand because if I tried to speak after that apology, I would've completely broken down.

There was a knock on the door—perfect timing, as far as I was concerned. That conversation went way better than expected. Time to quit while we were ahead. Billy poked her head in the room, Scott following behind her. Her smile fell as she glanced back and forth between me and my pop. "Hey, are we interrupting?"

I looked back at him, wondering if he was ready for this. I wanted things to change, but I wouldn't take his decision away or risk upsetting him.

"Nope," he said. "Maybe you and Scott oughta have a seat." He met my eyes, and I internally fist pumped when he gave me a slight smile. "I think there are some things we need to figure out."

COLE

Aiden's dad had been on the mend for the last two weeks. He still had some healing to do, but the doctor told him light exercise was good for him. He also said he could get back to regular activities like going out to eat for healthy meals—which is how we'd all ended up at SandBar on a Saturday afternoon, celebrating…well, a lot of things.

To see Aiden's face when his dad walked in SandBar's doors —for the first time in the three years it had been there—was a moment I was so happy to be a part of. I held Aiden's hand as Jim looked around, nodding his head in approval. He casually walked to the outside patio, tested the strength of the tables, checked the view as if the ocean hadn't always been there, came back inside, circled the bar. All the while, Aiden squeezed my hand watching his dad make a full inspection.

Jim stopped in front of Aiden, a crowd of Pointers anxiously watching and waiting as he rocked back on his heels and crossed his arms over his chest. Finally, he said impassively, "It'll do."

The broad smile that followed popped the bubble of tension floating in the room, a collective sigh releasing through the crowd. "It'll do *just* fine. Especially since my place will be gettin' a facelift to match."

"Excuse me…whose place?" Billy asked, cupping her hand to her ear.

"I'm still gonna be part owner," Jim argued, but when Billy didn't drop her hand, he added, "Okay, fine. *Our* place will be gettin' a facelift."

Billy patted him on the shoulder, an angelic smile aimed toward her uncle. "Now, was that so hard?"

"Well, I mean…" He rubbed a hand over his chest.

"That excuse is running dry, old man." Billy leaned in and kissed his cheek. "It's gonna be great, Uncle Jim. Just you wait and see."

"Bah." He swiped a hand at her but flashed her a proud smile. That smile carried over to Aiden. "I mean it, Aiden. You did good, son." Jim stretched his neck high, deliberately staring at a few Pointers. "I challenge any of y'all to disagree."

"I don't know…seems to me a local business owner, someone whose business we pour our money into, should at least be honest."

That fucking voice behind me shot down my spine like nails on a chalkboard. How had I ever found it sexy? Aiden and I turned to find Drake standing there, holding Pouty the Kid's hand. The poor guy looked uncomfortable, to say the least.

"You got something to say, Myers? Don't hold back on my account." Aiden pinned Drake with a look that said, *give it your best shot, asshole.*

"It's amazing how busy your bar is, Rafferty." Drake looked around, his smile taking on even more arrogance, if that was even possible. It was obvious he was living for the crowd around us growing in size. As usual with him, everything was better with an audience. "Tell me, is that why you and Cole lied about being together? Any gossip that brings people in to spend money in your bar, right?"

"You saying I made up a relationship with Cole to get business? Is that really what you're going with?" Aiden huffed, crossed his arms over his chest, and stared Drake down. But me? Yeah, I was fucking shitting a brick.

How the hell did Drake find out? I searched out my mom in the crowd, asking her with just my expression alone if she was responsible. She was the only one I'd told recently except for my dad, and he would never say a thing. But after my mom and I had cleared the air, I didn't think she was responsible, either. She shook her head, wringing her hands. Chatter grew louder around us as I looked around anxiously to see who'd caught her reaction. I glanced at Aiden, expecting to see disappointment. Instead, what I saw was encouragement so solid it gave me strength.

Burke, Levi, Ford, and Noah pushed through one side of the throng of people who were whispering and snickering. Sage came out of the crowd and took up his favorite spot, right next to Levi, aiming a glare at Drake so vicious I wasn't sure how it didn't knock Drake on his ass. From the other side, Jared, Billy, and her husband Scott took up defensive stances and equally hard stares.

"What's he talking about, Aiden?" Jim asked. I shut my eyes, cringing, my hands tightening into fists. Aiden and his dad were just getting back on good terms, and now this? This was all my fault.

"Yeah, why don't you tell them, Rafferty? Tell everyone how you used Cole and them to pad your own damn pockets," Drake snarled. "Tell them how you took it a step even farther and used that damn kiss at the festival as an excuse to make even more of a buzz."

"Are you fucking kidding me?" *Holy shit, did I just say that?* One minute I was staring at Drake, noticing how there was no one

even without any words. I felt his strength and light seep into my skin, filling me with warmth. I was able to take that light and turn it into my own words, and damn, did I have some things to say.

"My real relationship with Aiden? That one grew naturally, over weeks of spending time together, of him letting me know that I'm worth more, of him showing me that I matter in a way I never dreamed possible because you treated me like shit for so long." I took a deep breath. *Might as well throw it all out there.* "There's nothing fake about what we have now. I have *never* loved anyone the way I love Aiden." Aiden sucked in a breath next to me, his hand tightening on the nape of my neck, but I was terrified to meet his eyes. I did, however, meet the eyes of my four best friends, and they all nodded in approval and support.

"I'll be damned if anyone in this town is going to spew more shit about him." I glared at some of the guilty Pointers, who cowered under the scrutiny. *Yeah, how do you like it?* "I'm not even sure what the point of all this is. Public humiliation? Retaliation because Aiden told the town about your *shortcomings*?" The guys muffled laughs, Ford muttering an *oh shit*. "Or is it jealousy because, even when faking it, Aiden's a better boyfriend than you ever were?"

"One thing's for damn sure," Jim, of all people, spoke up. "This is my celebration of life, dammit, and you're not welcome to be a part of it." Drake looked fucking livid, Evian glared daggers at Drake, turning in a huff and stomping toward the exit, and Drake's parents? Well, I couldn't tell if they were embarrassed *for* their son or *because* of him. "Anyone who holds on to vile gossip, waiting for a big enough crowd to strike, is nothing but a creep in my book." Jim snorted. "No wonder your name rhymes with snake." He pointed at Aiden and let out a hearty chuckle. "You see what I did there?" Aiden and I both lost it, joined by most of the people in the crowd.

"Is that where you get it from?" I teased Aiden, but when his eyes met mine, I lost my breath. No one had ever looked at me the way he did.

I was completely caught up in Aiden's intense stare, but when he pulled me closer and said, "I love you, too," loud enough for the people around us to hear, everyone else faded away. He kissed me, right there in the middle of SandBar, not caring who saw us or what they thought.

Of course, if the catcalls were anything to go by…

Teresa swooned, "Sweet baby Jesus and all the saints in Heaven," making Aiden and me laugh against each other's mouths.

I pressed my face to his neck, breathing him in. Was it crazy to think he smelled different, more divine and intoxicating, now that he was mine? *So be it.*

Our friends and family circled around us, the rest of the people dispersing—or leaving, if they knew what was good for them.

Aiden wrapped his arms around my waist, his forehead leaning against mine. "The best thing I ever did was convince you to be in a fake relationship with me. You're amazing, you know that?"

"I know I'm really happy. The happiest I've ever been," I said softly.

Aiden sighed, pecking me on the lips. "Me, too. My pop's here, we're gonna get the ball rolling for the merge, and I really fucking love my boyfriend."

I laughed. "Sounds so right when you say it."

"Yeah, it does," he growled, kissing me again until my knees went weak. "So. Damn. Right."

EPILOGUE

COLE

Two months later...

"You finally agreed on a design, huh?" Levi asked Aiden, looking at the glass in his hand as he ran his fingers over the mockup of the new logo for Rafferty's SandBar.

Aiden sat down next to me, leaning in to kiss me before answering, "Finally. It's getting there. Between working here, getting the renovations done at Rafferty's Brewery, and being the referee between Billy and my pop, I'm tired as hell."

"Well, I mean...you have *some* energy leftover at the end of the day," I teased, wiggling my eyebrows.

Aiden's green eyes darkened, his mouth curving into a wicked smile. I knew exactly how wicked that delicious mouth could be. To say our last two months together had been active was an understatement. I was rarely home anymore, spending every night with Aiden at his place—much to Teresa's delight across the street. She sure kept the Walkie Talkies up to speed. Of course, if the woman really knew what we did behind closed doors, I guaran-fucking-tee she'd be too flustered to put it into words.

"Noah, they're doing it again," Burke complained.

Noah laughed. "What do you want me to do about it?"

"I don't know, but those of us not gettin' any shouldn't be subject to hearing about their damn sex life all the time." Burke took a big bite of his steak, moaning from the taste of it. There was nothing Burke respected more than a well-cooked meal.

Which reminded me… "Hey, Burke. Remember that *meal* we talked about months ago in my office?" I waited for Burke to look at me, his eyebrows drawn together in confusion. "Your taste buds would fucking explode."

Ford spewed his beer, Home of the Wave spraying all over his fries. He'd caught on quickly, especially since he was the one who'd started the whole thing about Aiden's ass that day.

Burke stared at me for another second, until recognition dawned and an approving smile turned that frown upside down. "Well, why didn't you say that in the first place?"

I barked out a laugh, along with Ford and Noah, Aiden…poor guy…looked completely confused, and Levi just shook his head.

"Hey," Sage said, coming over to our table with a tall, lanky guy behind him. Sage nudged my shoulder and gave me and Aiden a look then addressed the rest of the table. "Everyone, this is Baxter."

"'Sup," the guy drawled, his half-lidded eyes not focusing. Jeez, he was baked more than my grandma's burnt-bottom Christmas cookies.

Sage pointed to me first then went around the table. "Baxter, this is…Harold, Ernie, Larry, Pete, Milton, and Edgar."

Uh oh...H.E.L.P. M.E? I watched the guys as each one of them caught on. Sage had come up with a signal for us to jump in and save him from whatever bad date he was on at the time—

which was also why he only went out with them in Coral Pointe. It was sort of like a game for us trying to figure it out, even though Sage was not amused that he had to use it...*again*. There actually hadn't been a date yet where he didn't need it.

Aiden squeezed my thigh under the table. I bit my bottom lip, holding in my laugh. One of us needed to come up with an excuse or, as Sage so nicely put it months ago... "Jean Grey's gonna go all Phoenix on your asses if one of you X-men don't step in and save me."

Sage had given up waiting for Levi not long after Jim's heart attack. Maybe he realized waiting around for someone wasn't all it was cracked up to be, because I had a sneaking suspicion he'd figured out that Levi had feelings for Ford. Still, I couldn't help but think that what Sage felt for Levi went beyond unrequited love. That if Levi woke the hell up and figured out what he'd lost out on with Sage, he'd be kicking himself right now.

"Excuse me for a second..." Levi stood up and walked over to the far side of the bar, phone to his ear. Ironically, Sage's phone rang seconds later.

"Hey, Dad, what's up?" Sage met my eyes but quickly looked away when it was clear I was trying not to laugh. "The pipe burst? Oh no," he sighed. "But...I'm on a date." He looked back at Stoner Dude apologetically. "No, you're right. I can't let the house flood and make you lose all your worldly possessions. What kind of son would I be?" He dramatically covered his heart and shrugged at Stoner Dude, shaking his head.

Ford snorted, quickly covering it with a cough. Noah patted him on the back, but he wasn't holding up to this comedy routine any better.

"All right. I'll be there as soon as I can. Tell Mom I love her and to get on top of a high surface. You know the water will be up to her knees as fast as Burke burns a soufflé."

"Hey!" Burke griped, but Ford hit his arm hard. If Sage didn't end this call soon, we were all going to blow his cover. But, oh man…Burke's face…

"*Larry*, what's wrong?" Ford asked innocently. "Did you want to say something?"

Burke narrowed his eyes at him. "Oh, I don't know, *Pete*. I was just thinking I hope it's not as fast as our pal Ford Ferrari finishes on a first date."

"Well played," Ford nodded in approval. "You're dead to me."

Levi came back over to the table, giving us all a look but obviously trying as hard as us not to laugh. "What'd I miss?"

All five of us spoke at the same time… *Sage has to leave… Timmy fell in a well... Sage's parents need a raft... Burke burns his soufflés... Ford has no stamina...*

Levi looked at us for a second, nodded his head, then went back to eating his club sandwich.

Sage turned to Stoner Dude. "Well, it looks like I have to go. Thanks for the, uh…"—he patted his crossbody bag—"brownies." Turning to Aiden, he said, "I'm gonna use the back exit, 'k?" Without waiting another second, Sage walked across the bar, straight into Aiden's office. It was the best place for him to hide while looking through the one-way glass window to make sure the guy left.

"Whatever," the guy uttered, pulling a wrapped brownie out of his pocket as he walked away.

The second he was out the door, we all lost it. Sage waited another minute until the coast was clear then came back over to our table.

"What the actual fuck, Sage," Burke growled. "My soufflés are not burnt."

Sage shook his head patronizingly. "'Course not, big guy."

"I don't get it," Levi said. "Why do you keep going on these bad dates?"

Sage huffed at the man. "How am I supposed to know they're bad until I go on them?"

Levi tossed his napkin down, his brows pulling together. "There's gotta be a better way to meet someone than a dating app. I mean, come on, Sage…you're better than that. You deserve better than that."

Interesting…

Sage gave everyone else at the table an incredulous look. "Is he for real? Like…seriously?" He looked back at Levi. "You are the most… I can't even believe… Levi Hansen, you are unbelievable, you know that? Fucking unbelievable." Sage turned back to the table. "I'm going home."

Sage left in a huff, leaving Levi with his mouth gaping. "What'd I say?"

Collective groans rang out around the table, but Aiden was the one who spoke up and asked, "You really don't know?"

"Don't know what?"

"Dude, Sage has been trying to get *someone's* attention for over year. You really have no clue?" Ford looked at Levi like he had three heads.

Ford, if you only knew…

Levi threw his hands in the air. "Would somebody tell me what y'all are talking about? What guy?"

Noah held his hand up to silence us, then simply said, "*Edgar*." He locked eyes with Levi and we all waited.

"Wha—" Levi stopped abruptly, his eyebrows rising to his hairline as he looked at each one of us. "*Edgar?*" he whispered.

Burke rolled his eyes. "There it is. Hello, epiphany. Welcome to the conversation."

"But…" Levi opened and closed his mouth again. He was gonna need to sit with that one for a bit.

"On that note, there's a boat…needs docking," Aiden said to me, his eyebrows wiggling.

"Hell yeah," I rasped back, pushing up from the table.

Everyone but Levi and Burke laughed, Burke grumbling, "We know what that means now. Don't think you're slick."

I held up a finger, a wicked grin on my face. "We will be slick in a—"

"Okay! Time to go!" Aiden grabbed my hand yanking me toward the door. I could hear the guys laughing behind me, but my mind only cared about one thing: Aiden was mine, for the rest of my life—and I loved being the place he dropped his anchor.

The End.

Want more Cole and Aiden?
Join my readers' group, where I'll be posting a sexy bonus scene soon!!
Quinn's Cove

OTHER BOOKS BY JACLYN QUINN

Haven's Cove Series in order:

Hard to Let Go

Hard to Get

Hard to Hold

Beyond the Cove Series (Haven's Cove Spinoff) in order:

Drawn to You (Brighton Pier)

Thirst for You (Riverside Falls)

Appeal to You (Brighton Pier)

Fight for You (Riverside Falls)

Road to You (Brighton Pier)

Standalones:

Bet on It

Spreadsheets

A Taste of Christmas

AUTHOR'S NOTE

Reviews are always appreciated and really help to get my name out there! If you've enjoyed my books, please consider putting a review on Amazon and Goodreads. Thanks!

If you'd like to keep up with me and future releases, join my Facebook readers' group:

Quinn's Cove

I'd love to hear from you! Here are all my SM links. You can find me on Facebook, Instagram, and Twitter.

Follow Me! links

ACKNOWLEDGMENTS

Thanks so much to my alpha readers Jenn, Star, and Steph! You help me more than you could possibly know and keep me going from chapter to chapter! Thank you to my beta readers Mere, Luna, and Riley! I appreciate you taking the time to read and help make my baby the best it can be!! Anita, thank you so much for helping me get rid of all the things that would make a reader go *huh*? You're an amazing editor. Never doubt it! Allison, as always, thank you for being the last eyes on my book, making sure I didn't miss anything! Morningstar, you are rocking these covers. You know I'm in love with them all!!

ABOUT THE AUTHOR

I have been an artist from a very young age. From drawing cartoon characters and evolving into portraits, making jewelry, photography, and now writing. I have an amazing support system in my family and friends and couldn't be more grateful!

I live in central New Jersey, love summers at the Jersey Shore, rock music, wine, sexy men, and laughing a lot with my amazing friends and family. Sunday dinners at my parents' house are crazy, hysterical, and you can count on a movie quote…or ten…being thrown out. Insults between siblings is how we show our love for each other!

When I'm not creating, you can find me reading books from my favorite authors. I'm a hopeless romantic, starving for passionate characters, and always craving that happy ending, whether in reading or in writing my own books. Of course, I always make time for ghost videos on YouTube and true crime shows, too. LOL

Made in the USA
Middletown, DE
02 April 2025

73543483R00125